DAWN OF THE QUEEN

A
CYCLE OF AWAKENING
NOVELLA

ANDREW STEVENS

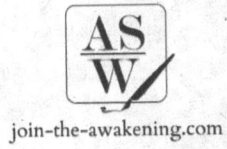

join-the-awakening.com

SAH'NARA

'ISA

NORTHREACH

LONELY PINES

THE VALE

JEB'S POST

VALEHOLD

SOLANTRIA

SOLHARBOR

ONG ISLE

Copyright © 2025 by Andrew Stevens
Cover design by Rachel St. Clair
Cover illustration by Sutthiwat Dechakampu
Map by Andrew Stevens, design elements by Rachel St. Clair
Author photograph by Douglas Brauner

Self-published by Andrew Stevens
P.O. Box 25402
Colorado Springs, CO 80936
https://join-the-awakening.com

First edition: July 2025

ISBNs:
979-8-9929519-2-9 (ebook)
979-8-9929519-3-6 (trade paperback)

To my wife...

We have weathered many storms. You have put up with my passion, and on occasion, pulled me down when my head soared a little too far above the clouds. You are the line that grounds me, the light that guides me through, and the love that makes it all worthwhile. I couldn't be who I truly am without you. Never stop believing how much you mean to me.

To my past self...

We always knew we had these gifts, but it took some time to learn how to dedicate them to a project and see it through. We struggled to believe, and we wasted our time doing so many things that didn't really matter. But we did it, we finally did it, and this is just the beginning.

To the believers...

Mom, Dad, Alane, John, and all the others. You know who you are. You believed in me, you believed in my gifts. You'll never truly know how much of a difference that made. Thank you!

To the dreamers and creatives...

You have a gift. Don't settle for anything less than using it to the fullest. Don't let your future self regret the years wasted. Reach for the stars, take the leap. There's no better time than right now.

CONTENTS

PROLOGUE

Dragons

Long before the Age of Men, there was a time when dragons ruled the heavens above and the lands below. They were the first of the creations in Velasia, ultimately given the task of protecting the world as its stewards–a task appointed to them by the now vanished gods known only as the Architects.

Since the creation of time, the dragons served this purpose faithfully. Though not all was perfect, there was balance. However, as the seasons shift, so too did the dragons' supremacy come to an end.

But unlike the seasons, it was not a subtle change.

Long ago, men, the least of all the sentient species, served only as slaves to the ancient, magical races of Velasia. But thousands of years ago, all that changed. And with that change, so too did the balance of power slowly begin to shift. But that is another tale entirely. However, as change came upon Velasia and men grew in power, so too did the dragons desire to rise up yet again as the true lords of the world.

And it was in this time when one dragon reached too far...

For as long as dragons lived, the Wyrmlords sat in the seat of power in Dor'Dragos–the very heart of the dragon empire. Alongside these wyrms, their dragonesses served faithfully. But when one such Wyrmlord, Dro'Kal, the last of the male rulers, grew greedy in his dominion, everything changed.

Posthumously named the Worldeater, Dro'Kal's greed saw him nearly sunder the world in two. Devouring most of Velasia's magical fonts of power, his exploits led to the diminishing of the other ancient races, further propelling the rise of men as the dominant species.

Dro'Kal would have nearly succeeded in this task, and likely destroyed the world, if it weren't for the dragonesses who rose up to challenge him.

This is the story of that uprising. This is the story of the dragoness who rose to lead a rebellion, igniting the fires of change, and bringing about a new dawn–the Dawn of the Queen.

Chapter One

LIOTHA

Liotha sat silently, watching several younglings frolic about the courtyard from the shadows of her balcony. Her hand went to her stomach, resting there for a moment. She could feel the presence of the extra magic there now. Her own younglings would greet the world in about a cycle.

She'd only just realized quite recently that she was expecting. During most of the first term, she'd still be able to take human form, but after that it would be her true form for the remainder. Though some didn't approve, Liotha rather liked her human form. Plus, it made it easier to manage around her home. Her husband, Hel'aren, was a Drae'tar in the Wyrmsguard, working his way up the ranks, trying to get into Dro'Kal's circle. If he did, they might be moved to a larger residence. But for now, their humble home served its purpose well enough. Liotha just hoped they would be able to move before she needed more space. Her husband said he was close to bending Dro'Kal's ear in his favor.

Liotha smiled and stood, coming up to the balcony's edge, basking in the warmth of the sun as it graced her skin. She enjoyed hearing the laughter of the innocent younglings playing in the courtyard, imagining what her own would do when they joined the others below. She wondered how many she would have.

Her good friend Kel'ana had laid eleven, though three of them didn't make it. It was a sad fact of life, but it was quite normal for not all the eggs to hatch. Either way, Liotha hoped it would be at least six or seven.

Turning away from the scene outside, she came in and looked around, imaging half a dozen younglings running about the place.

"Definitely not enough room..." she sighed, shaking her head.

There wasn't much they had in the way of belongings. After all, it had just been the two of them for two cycles now. Despite that, she had the sudden urge to organize and move things around. She began with rearranging some of the furniture on the wall next to the balcony exit. There were two narrow, wooden tables that held several heirlooms Liotha's family had given them when she and Hel'aren were mated.

Liotha picked up one of the items, a pearlescent glass orb with the shards of Liotha's own egg inside, holding it up as she stared at it warmly. It was a tradition in most dragon families to preserve the pieces of the egg inside a glass orb as a memento. Liotha's mother always had been one for tradition.

Liotha carefully picked up the orb's stand and set both off to the side, resting them gently on the sofa where they would be safe while she moved things. She turned back, starting to slide the table sideways when she heard a knock at the front door.

When she opened the door, she was greeted by the beaming face of Kel'ana.

"Liotha! My, aren't you looking glowing. It doesn't take long, does it?"

"Hello, Kel'ana. Good to see you, too. And yes, I can feel it. It's so surreal!"

"Oh, you don't know the half of it. Just wait until the second term. It will feel like mini lightning strikes pulsing through your belly."

"So I've heard. But anyway, come inside. What do I owe the pleasure of this visit?"

"I wanted to stop by and see if you still wanted to go to that gathering tonight. It's not for a few hours, but I'm going to do a little shopping first since we'll be down near the main market," Kel'ana rambled as she entered and looked around, her eyes landing on furniture Liotha was still in the process of moving.

"Already got the itch, I see," she added, tilting her head to the side.

Liotha's eyes followed, remembering the table.

"Ah, yes," she said, her pale skin turning several shades redder. She moved over to the table and gently pushed it back into place. "You mentioned the gathering," she said, turning back to Kel'ana, trying to change the subject. "What's it about again?"

Kel'ana looked around curiously, leaning forward. Liotha, confused, shot her friend a questioning look. Kel'ana took a few steps closer.

"Just a bunch of us mothers—and a few *saureen*, like yourself—getting together to gossip. There have been rumors that..." she paused, looking around again, "that there has been trouble outside our borders."

"Trouble?" Liotha questioned, twisting her brow. "What kind of trouble?"

"I'm not sure, exactly, but we'll find out more tonight. Will you come with me?"

"Sure, I suppose I can come. After all, Hel'aren said he'd probably be home late again. He's been working extra time to try to get ahead of the others. The Selection is in two weeks and he's hopeful he will be promoted to Drae'vir."

"Ah, how excellent. I'm sure he'll be selected. He's been working so hard!"

"Yes..." Liotha acknowledged, her mouth drawn out in a line before smiling again. "He has been working hard. I guess a night out would do me some good."

"Excellent. I have to go make sure the house is in order and the caretaker is prepared for my absence. I'll stop back by in about two hours. Make sure you're ready!" Kel'ana called out as she disappeared through the doorway and into the narrow street in front of Liotha's home.

Liotha closed the door, turning back to her task at hand.

"Right. So, an hour to work on this mess and then I'll start getting ready. Better get to it."

Two hours later, nearly on the dot, Kel'ana returned. Liotha greeted her wearing a light evening gown, which shimmered with a teal hue. It was a simple dress, but slightly fancier than what she normally wore. She figured this was a special enough occasion.

Kel'ana was dressed similarly, though Liotha could tell by the look of her gown that it was more expensive than her own. Kel'ana's husband worked for the High Council, making his pay and station a good bit higher than Liotha's mate. Liotha tried not to let it bother her.

"Oh, you look ravishing, Liotha!" Kel'ana belauded.

"Not as nearly as you," Liotha replied, blushing.

"Oh, this old thing? You're too kind. Well, are you ready to go then?"

"Yes, let's," Liotha answered, following Kel'ana out the front door, turning around for one last look to survey her final rearrangement.

The two of them meandered down the narrow street and out toward the central byway of the northern sector of Dor'Dragos. The byways were large open spaces where dragons could assume their true forms, stretching their wings for flight.

Here, in the northern section of the city, the byways were busy, but not like the crowded byways of the southern sections of the capital, where the commoners lived and worked. As Liotha's mate was a member of the Royal Guard, they had been allowed to claim a small abode in this section of the city. Liotha was glad, as the southern sections were generally less desirable.

As the two of them came out into the open air, they looked at each other, knowing they would need to take flight to reach the capital's main market in the heart of the city. In a shimmer of magical energy, they both assumed their true forms. Liotha was about average size for a female. She had vibrant scales, with shades of purple and green shimmering along her spine, ending in a grey-blue hue along her sides and onto her belly. Her crown of horns sat neatly on her head, leading to gentle slope of spikes down her back. Her eyes, one of her most prominent features, glowed in shades of purple—a rarity, even among dragons. Though all dragons have glowing eyes—a direct testament of the magic flowing through their bodies—variations of red, yellow, and orange were the most common.

Kel'ana, on the other hand, had yellow eyes and a bright yellow spine, fading quickly to a black underbelly. Her coloration was not as regal as Liotha's, though she was a good bit larger in stature.

As the two of them rose into the air, relishing in the wind beneath their wings, they smiled at each other before aiming south toward Dor'Dragos's central sector. To reach this section, they would have to land early and enter through the Gates of Iteria, otherwise risk the wrath of the Skyguard. The skies above the city's heart, where the palace sat, were strictly off-limits except for the royal family and those who directly served them.

Liotha aimed for the gate, but noticed Kel'ana wasn't diving. She shot her a questioning look.

"We're not going to the Royal Market, today. Sorry, I must have forgotten to mention it. We're going to Mundalis Square. The meeting is down there, and I haven't been in some time, so I figured we'd check out the goods the commoners are peddling these days."

"Oh, I see."

"Is that alright?"

"Yes, of course..." Liotha replied, though the thought made her a bit nervous. If the meeting was being held in the southern sector, that was a bit more concerning as well. What was this meeting actually about?

Liotha snapped out of her thoughts, noticing Kel'ana had shifted her direction and was flying more southwest, meaning to avoid the skies of the central sector. Liotha followed, catching back up and matching speed.

It didn't take them long to reach the southern section. The border guards watched as they flew over the walls dividing both the north and western sections, and once again as they made their way into the southern skies. Traveling south wasn't so much of an issue, but when they went back north, they'd likely be harassed by the guards, needing to provide proof of residence and permission to cross to the upper sectors.

They quickly spotted the southern byway, which was, as Liotha expected, crowded and bustling with activity. They landed as best they could, trying to avoid bumping into the dozens of dragons coming or going in their direct vicinity. Still, Liotha wasn't used to having this little space, and she accidentally brushed up against a particularly large drake who was preparing for liftoff.

"Watch where you're going, *puella*" he called out in a gruff tone, using the derogatory term for female dragons. He eyed Liotha up and down as she shifted back into her human form.

"Watch your tone, commoner," Kel'ana retorted, still in her dragon form, almost matching the drake's own size. They stared each other down for a moment, Liotha backing up, unsure what was about to happen.

The drake finally scoffed, eyeing Liotha one last time before spreading his wings and lifting off. Kel'ana watched him leave, then shifted back into her own human skin alongside Liotha.

"Wretched commoners. Of course, I'd be grumpy all the time too if I had to live down here. I can already smell the stink."

Liotha smirked but was more rattled by the chance encounter than Kel'ana was. Her friend had always been strong-willed–something that only grew even more so once she'd become a mother.

Liotha hurried after Kel'ana, who was already making her way down the street that led to the main city market. Following, Liotha quickly forgot about the previous encounter as she marveled at the enormity of this section of the city. The southern section was at least four times the size of the northern section, and it was crammed with at least ten times the inhabitants, if not more. As such, rows of houses stacked one on top of each other, extending as far as Liotha could see down the side streets. Most of them were even smaller than her own, but there were others, probably owned by rich merchants and business drakes, who lived more luxuriously.

There was a steady stream of all types of dragons, most in their human forms, moving up and down the streets, along with constant shadows cast from those flying overhead.

When they turned a corner and came into the outer section of the market, the dull hum of the streets grew to an intense roar. It grew even more crowded, so much so that Liotha couldn't help but bump into someone every few seconds. Down here, everyone was in their human form. There would be no room, otherwise.

It was then that the smells wrested Liotha's attention.

She recognized many of the scents – roasted meats of all types, baked fruits, candies, and various other food aromas, all with a strong undertone of ale. There were other scents she did not know, presumably exotic spices and perfumes from beyond their borders. While they had such things at the Royal Market, the selection was much more curated, and generally varied little. But down here, you never knew what you might find.

It was all a bit overwhelming. Liotha focused on her friend, sticking as close as she could manage. Kel'ana looked back every now and then but continued to trudge through the constant flow of bodies, seemingly on a mission to get somewhere specific, and seeming much less fixated on the sights and sounds around them.

They spent more than an hour stopping by various stalls, examining goods, and heckling merchants, though it was Kel'ana doing most of it. Liotha didn't have much mind to buy anything, though there were a few items she pondered. She and Hel'aren were saving at the moment, so she mostly just watched Kel'ana interacting with the various shop owners.

Eventually, Kel'ana admitted she'd had enough, noting the gathering was happening soon, and was off again, heading out of the market, Liotha at her heels as they twisted through streets she'd never been on before. The streets grew less crowded, which Liotha wasn't sure she liked. While it had been overwhelming in the market, it was easy to blend in there. Here, the stares she got began to gnaw at the nape of her neck, making her feel uncomfortable.

After what felt like ages, they came at last to a quiet section of a street that terminated in a dead end. At its conclusion sat a small tavern, a sign painted above with the words 'The Well'. There were a few shady-looking individuals outside, but otherwise, it was mostly quiet.

Inside, it was much the same.

As they entered, Liotha felt a further prick on the back of her neck. She eyed the few patrons sitting about various tables, several of them eyeing her back. Kel'ana was headed straight for the bar. The barkeep behind the counter weighed the two of them, her gaze moving up and down in an assessing manner, especially as her eyes landed on Liotha.

"What can I get for you two?" she asked as Liotha and Kel'ana came up to the edge of the counter.

Kel'ana paused, her eyes shifting as she leaned in a bit closer.

"We've come for a drink of the well..." she whispered.

The barkeep's eyes shifted to Liotha, then back to Kel'ana.

"She's with me. I vouch for her," Kel'ana added.

The barkeep nodded, lifting a section of the counter, motioning with her head for the two of them to pass. Hesitantly, Liotha followed Kel'ana as she passed beyond the counter and entered a shadowed doorway in the back, pushing aside a black curtain and continuing down a long hallway.

There were several storerooms off to the side, most of them filled with casks of what Liotha could only assume were ale or other such spirits. At the end of this hallway sat a red door, a stark contrast to the rest of the hallway. Kel'ana opened it and stepped through, beginning her descent of a staircase that wound down, curving out of sight. After descending a few steps, she stopped and turned backwards, noticing Liotha still waiting at the top.

"It's alright. I've been here before. There's nothing to fear."

Liotha swallowed, unconvinced. Not wanting to get left behind, she slowly began to step downward.

After several dozen steps, they arrived at the bottom and quickly found their way out into a large open room, surrounded on all sides by damp, stone walls lined with lit torches. There was a fire pit in the center of the room, around which sat at least two dozen dragonesses of various attire. Liotha thought she recognized at least a few of them.

"Ah, Kel'ana, you made it. We were afraid we'd have to start without you," greeted an elder dragoness with black hair, streaks of silver running through it. Her cheekbones were sharp, her nose sharper. Her piercing, emerald-colored eyes moved to Liotha. "And who is it that you have brought this time?"

"Hail, Mother Ere'daina," Kel'ana offered, bowing. "This is my good friend, Liotha. Her husband is a Drae'tar in the Royal Guard. I thought she would benefit from this conclave's knowledge."

Kel'ana turned to Liotha, extending her hand. Liotha stepped forward and took it.

"Liotha, this is Mother Ere'daina, Scion of Shaetalis," Kel'ana said as she handed Liotha's hand towards the dragoness.

Scion of Shaetalis! Liotha's eyes widened as the words left her friend's mouth.

Shaetalis was one of the thirteen ruling bloodlines of the dragon kingdom. As Scion, that meant she sat on the High Council. Liotha had seen plenty of council members before, but she'd never been introduced to one directly. It also meant she was only one of two dragonesses on the High Council, which was primarily disclosed of drakes.

"Mother Ere'daina," Liotha offered, bowing. "It's an honor to meet you. I had no idea Kel'ana was bringing me into such esteemed company."

A disquieting smile pursed the older dragoness's lips, her head dipping in acknowledgement.

"That is kind of you, *saureen*. Though, not for much longer it seems."

"You can tell?" Liotha asked, a bit taken aback.

"Yes. Only a few weeks by my guess, correct?"

"Why... yes, actually. I only just realized a few days ago."

"Well then, congratulations are in order. There is no greater honor than being a mother. I hope it serves you well."

Liotha smiled and bowed again, feeling a bit awkward with everyone in the room watching their exchange.

"But enough with greetings. You two may find a seat. It's time we get started..." Ere'daina noted, waving her hand toward several open chairs. Liotha and Kel'ana quickly found their seats as all eyes turned to the elder Mother.

"As most of you know, there have been reports from beyond our borders, indicating trouble amongst the other races," Ere'daina started, followed by nods from most in attendance. "For some time, these have only been rumors. However, I decided to send my scouts out to see if there was any truth to these claims. And what I have found is... disturbing, to say the least. It would seem many of the fonts of power throughout the extended kingdoms have somehow dried up."

Gasps echoed throughout the chamber. Liotha's eyes grew wide, trying to process what had just been said.

"How is that possible?" asked the dragoness directly to Liotha's right.

"How indeed..." Ere'daina replied, her eyes grazing Liotha for a brief second before moving about the rest. "I believe Dro'Kal is at the heart of it."

More gasps filled the room as everyone exchanged concerned looks.

"What are you implying?" Liotha asked, quickly growing uncomfortable.

"I'm not implying anything, my dear. My scouts have been watching the borders, monitoring the comings and goings of Dro'Kal and his cohorts. Their trips have grown more frequent, often carried out in secret. And every time they return, a new report comes in shortly thereafter of another font drying up. This is no coincidence."

"What does this mean, exactly?" asked another dragoness. "Why would he do such a thing?"

"Why else," Ere'daina asked the group. She paused, waiting for a response. "We have all had the thought before. If only we had an unlimited source of power, maybe we could circumvent these... limitations placed upon us by our creators. To live forever in our true forms. Isn't that the aspiration of all our kind?"

"Yes, but it's not really possible... is it?" the dragoness asked. Liotha's mind raced as she processed what Mother Ere'daina was getting at.

"Theoretically," Liotha said, her mind still racing. She didn't notice all eyes move to her, a silence falling over the room "If one was able to absorb enough magic, it might be enough to override the limitation. But there's no way to know for sure without trying. But that exactly what Dro'Kal is trying to do, isn't it?" Liotha was fascinated by the thought, but the idea was madness.

"Precisely," said Mother Ere'daina, giving Liotha a nod. "If we don't stop him, he could consume all the world's magic. And the repercussions of that could prove disastrous."

Small talk and further questions spread throughout the room. Liotha leaned closer to her friend.

"Why did you bring me here? This is dangerous talk," Liotha whispered to Kel'ana. "We could be arrested–or worse–just for being here."

"Liotha..." Kel'ana whispered back, a disquieting smirk etched across her lips. "You can't be so naïve to what's happening around you. I know your mate is trying to get on Dro'Kal's good side, but is that really what you want? Is it worth it to live in a bigger house if the wyrm he serves destroys our world?"

"Isn't your mate–"

"Yes. And he's aware of what's going on. He's trying to get the others to open their eyes. Dro'Kal is not the wyrm he once was. He's changed, and not in a good way. He's too dangerous to continue to sit on the throne."

"Do you have something to share with the group, Kel'ana?" Mother Ere'daina questioned.

"I was just trying to explain to Liotha why Dro'Kal should no longer sit on the throne. Why he must be removed from power."

"And what does Liotha think of this? I'm sure this comes as quite the surprise."

Liotha's face continued to portray her disbelief and inner turmoil. She wanted to respond, but didn't quite know how to formulate the words. Slowly, she raised her head, exchanging gazes with everyone before focusing on Ere'daina.

"I had no idea what this meeting was going to be about. Kel'ana only told me it was just going to be gossiping, but if I had known, I wouldn't have come. What you're talking about is treason! Maybe Dro'Kal isn't himself; maybe what you say is true, but he's... he's our Wyrmlord. He commands the armies–he commands my mate. How can we–?" Liotha couldn't finish her thought, tears beginning to well in her eyes. She reached down and placed her hand over her stomach, bowing her head.

An awkward silence filled the room for a minute before Ere'daina stood, taking a deep breath.

"Yes, it is true. What we are talking about is technically treason. I know you are scared–we're all scared. But we cannot ignore the fact that the world may not survive if Dro'Kal is allowed to continue on his present course. Think of your children. What kind of world do you want to bring them up in, if there is even a world left should he continue this course."

Liotha raised her head, looking Ere'daina in the eye.

"If we don't act soon, then I fear for *all* our futures. The other races are, in fact, suffering greatly. Dro'Kal's greed will not stop with them. It's only a matter of time before his eyes turn inward to our own realms. And by then, he may be unstoppable. But right now, we still have a chance. However slim, we must seize it before it is too late."

Ere'daina turned her attention back to the rest of the room. Some of them still looked a bit concerned, while others were more moved by Ere'daina's words

"If we are to stand a chance, we're going to need all the help we can get. I am depending on all of you to lead this rebellion, recruiting others to our cause. But you must take care. The wyrms are cunning. The only advantage we have is they will not suspect us to challenge them. Too long have we sat idly by while the wyrms lead. It is our time to rise."

Ere'daina paused one more time, looking each attendee in the eye. When her eyes landed on Liotha, Liotha could not hold her gaze. Ere'daina frowned but continued on.

"So, will you join me? Will each of you do your part to prevent the annihilation of our people? Of the world?"

Slowly, the dragonesses in attendance stood, bowing to Mother Ere'daina and offering their pledges to the cause. She greeted each, placing her hand on their shoulder, offering specific words of encouragement, and bidding them to go.

When the last of them left, only Kel'ana and Liotha remained. Kel'ana shared a short gaze with Liotha, then stood and approached Ere'daina, doing as the others had. Liotha listened to their conversation, her eyes wide in contemplation as she processed what she herself was going to do.

"I'm proud of you, Kel'ana. You and your mate. If we are to succeed, we're going to need some of the drakes on our side as well. Just tell your mate to be careful, and not to do anything rash until we decide what to do."

"Yes, Mother," Kel'ana dipped her head. "What about–?" she asked, her eyes shooting sideways to Liotha.

"I'll speak to her. Go ahead and wait upstairs. I'll send her up shortly."

Kel'ana bowed again, glancing back at Liotha before heading up the stairs. Liotha watched her go, wishing desperately that she could go with her. But she was too scared to get up as Ere'daina moved to sit beside her. The older dragoness's presence didn't feel malicious, but there was still something unsettling about it.

"You know, I've only ever seen eyes like yours once before, a long time ago."

Liotha lifted her head, a curious expression forming.

"Her name was Zareena. When we were young, she and I were inseparable. We grew up next door to each other and met when we were just barely into our eleventh cycles. I don't remember what happened on the day we met, but I remember those eyes. They shone brighter than any I'd ever seen before," Ere'daina paused, smiling, a genuine sense of fondness behind it.

"Her spirit was also bright. She exceeded me in every way in our schooling. She exceeded everyone, but she never let it show. She was humble and kind... much like you, from what I can tell. I see the same tenderness behind your eyes."

Ere'daina held Liotha's gaze for a few seconds, her smile fading into a look of sadness.

"When we were nearing our eighty-second cycle, Zareena found out she was to be betrothed to a wyrm who'd just been appointed a seat on the High Council. He was two and a half times her age, but Zareena, being the good *saureen* that she was, she went along with it, though I knew she did not want to join her blood to his. I tried to convince her to break it off. I told her we could leave and go somewhere far away where they'd never find us. The world is a big place. How hard could it be for two dragons to find a place to settle down?" There was a deep sadness and a sense of regret in her tone.

"She would not leave. She would not admit her true feelings... She said it was her duty to her family–that being the mate of a High Councilor could afford her the opportunity to help others. Little did she know, she would get no such chance."

"I found out several weeks after the Joining. I hadn't heard from her, so I snuck out one night and went to her new home. When I found her, she was barely alive, the light in her eyes almost faded. Turns out this Councilor had an insatiable thirst for power. And Zareena, with her untapped potential, was nothing more than a target for his greed. He'd nearly drained her dry, trying to use it in a dark ritual known as *prae'natalis*–the transfusion of power by consuming blood."

Liotha's eyes grew wide in understanding.

"I was enraged. When I found him asleep in his bed, her blood still on his lips, I slit his throat, soaking the bed with the taint in his veins. I tried to take it back to Zareena. I tried to save her, but by the time I got back, she was minutes from her end. I have never wept so deeply as that night, watching her light fade into darkness."

"The next day, I heard the news that they'd found the bodies. Being a Councilor, they made up some ridiculous story about her killing him in his sleep and then committing suicide. They defiled her name and shamed her family. Only I knew the secret–a secret I have kept, not telling a soul... until you, that is."

"Why me?" Liotha asked, clearly puzzled. "You barely even know me."

"As I said, I see the same light in your eyes. I see the same potential to change the world. I spent all this time, devoted my entire life to making sure monsters like him would never hurt anyone I cared about ever again. The problem was, I became so ambitious, rising to be the first dragoness to sit on the High Council, I lost everything else along the way." There was a deep sadness in Ere'daina's words, reinforced by the distant look in her eyes. "I never found love again. I harbored too much hate to let any light in. And so, my purpose was all that fueled me–all that kept me going all these years."

"I knew Dro'Kal had the same greed and lust for power when I first met him. It came on slowly, but I watched it grow steadily. I had little fight left in me, fighting monsters like him all these years. I knew I had to do something but wasn't sure I had the strength to do it. At least, not until I laid eyes on you."

"When you walked through that doorway, a flood of memories came back. Of Zareena, of that night, of everything I've fought for all these years. I may not be the dragoness I once was. I know I can never go back to her. But you... you can be something far greater. You can be what Zareena should have been—what I attempted to become. With the power I see inside you, you can change the world in ways I never could."

"I know this is a lot for you to process. For that, I am sorry. But we are desperate. Something must be done to stop Dro'Kal, or I fear he will become the undoing of us all. Do you understand?"

Liotha sat silently. The voices in her head were screaming. She tried to focus on one train of thought, but it was too hard to process at the moment. She started to feel the room spinning.

"You don't have to say anything right now. You look like you could use some fresh air. Let's get you upstairs."

Ere'daina helped Liotha to her feet, holding her arm as they ascended the stairs. When they came out into the tavern, Liotha saw Kel'ana waiting for her. Her expression turned to concern, and she came over to grab Liotha's arm.

"Is everything okay?" she asked.

"She'll be fine," Ere'daina reassured her. "She just has a lot to process. Why don't you see her home."

Kel'ana nodded and they started to leave.

"Liotha," Ere'daina added. "Your mate cannot know of any of this. You understand why, of course?"

Liotha's eyes glazed over for a few seconds. She slowly turned her head back toward Ere'daina and nodded, feeling like she was going to be sick to her stomach. Kel'ana started walking again, keeping Liotha up as they exited the main entrance.

"So, what was all that about?" the dragoness behind the bar asked.

"She's the one who's going to lead this rebellion of ours," Mother Ere'daina replied.

"Her?"

"Yes," Ere'daina chuckled. "Her. She just doesn't know it yet. But it might take a little push in the right direction."

The smile faded from Ere'daina's face. Her eyes flickered as she stared coldly out into the dark streets of Dor'Dragos, watching the forms of Liotha and Kel'ana disappear into the night.

CHAPTER TWO

PUSH

Liotha awoke suddenly, sweat on her brow. She'd slept awfully, her night riddled with dreams of a past she did not know, of the girl with violet eyes, just like Mother Ere'daina had described. She'd also dreamt of the future, where she walked streets of fire, blood splattered on the walls, screams all around her. The ghosts of the things yet to come, perhaps.

Liotha tried to calm her nerves, convincing herself they were only dreams. Fortunately, the sun was already up, which helped her calm down further. She glanced beside her and noticed Hel'aren was already gone. *Out early and home late. Every day lately...*

She threw the covers off and hopped out of bed, heading to the kitchen to pour herself a glass of water. The jug emptied as she filled her cup, dripping to a halt before it reached the brim. She'd have to refill it at the community well before starting her day. For some reason, she felt absolutely parched.

Liotha downed the half-full glass of water and returned to her room to put on something more appropriate. When Hel'aren was promoted, perhaps the house they'd move into would have its own running water. She sighed dreamily, reaching for a standard light dress that shimmered with a dark purple sheen.

If only it were sooner. They said I'd need to drink more water when I carried, but this... this is exhausting.

Carrying the dress with her, she stepped in front of the small mirror hanging on the wall beside her bed. She gazed into her own eyes, her hand reaching up and gently caressing her cheek. She knew purple was rare, but could it really be more than just a color?

Liotha tore her gaze away from the mirror, forcing herself to focus on the task at hand. She quickly slipped into her dress and headed back to the kitchen, finding the jug and hoisting it against her chest with two hands, heading for the front door. Even empty, it was a bit heavy.

Outside, she navigated the side street and carefully exited into the main road leading toward the central byway, entering the steady drum of foot traffic, sticking to the side of the walkway to avoid bumping into anyone.

The well wasn't far—just the next street down and around the corner, but the trek was difficult with the heavy jug, and of course, even worse once it was full. She'd managed fine so far, but even though she was barely a few weeks carrying, she could already feel it weighing on her, sapping her own strength to nurture the miracles inside. She wondered for how long she'd be able to keep this up.

Liotha sighed and pressed onward, rounding the corner and coming into view of the well. There were a few other dragonesses gathered around it, some of whom Liotha recognized. She wasn't particularly friendly with any of them, but as they all shared a common burden, it was a bond they embraced politely.

Not feeling her normal socialness, Liotha merely smiled and nodded to the others as she approached, quickly setting about her task of filling the jug. Fortunately, it was slow enough at the moment that she didn't have to wait. There had been times when she had to wait her turn for almost an hour. Liotha sighed again just thinking about it. She was sighing a lot lately, it seemed.

When the first bucket came up, she contemplated drinking straight from it, as she was still so thirsty. But that was considered unsanitary, and Liotha didn't want to get looks from the others, so she dumped it in the jug and continued, licking her dry lips.

It took maybe ten minutes until the jug was full enough to her liking. She could have added one or two more buckets, but she was feeling a bit weak and worried about the walk back. So, she set the bucket back and wrapped her arms around the jug, lifting it with a grunt. She smiled one more time at the others, who were eyeing her, before turning and heading back down the street.

As Liotha rounded the corner, she came face to face with her mate.

"Hel'aren," Liotha exclaimed, trying not to spill any of the water.

"There you are!" Hel'aren puffed, an annoyed expression written across his face. "We need to go."

"Go? Go where?"

"The Council has requested our presence at an urgent assembly. We need to leave immediately. I don't want to be late!"

"What? Why would the Council—"

"I don't know, but it doesn't sound good. Come on, let's go."

"I need to get the water back..."

"Forget the water. This is more important. Just leave it."

"But we only have two jugs. I don't want to—"

"I said leave it!" Hel'aren shouted, drawing curious glances from several onlookers.

Stunned and a bit hurt by her mate's reaction, Liotha carefully began to set the jug down on the corner of the building nearby. She was already struggling from holding it, so she moved slowly, trying not to spill the water as she placed it down next to a nearby building.

Hel'aren, impatient with her speed, grabbed her arm and pulled her out into the street before she got the jug fully settled on the ground. Because of this, it toppled and tipped over, slamming into the ground with a smash, water spilling out into the street.

More stares joined the chorus of attention from everyone nearby, causing Liotha to blush. She looked back toward the other dragonesses at the well, all of them staring and whispering to each other. She took one last look at the cracked jug and spilt water, tears forming in her eyes. Looking back at her mate, he didn't seem to even care. He was just pulling her toward the byway, a solid grip on her arm. He'd never treated her like this. Whatever was going on must be serious.

Liotha turned her attention back forward and tried to forget about the jug, suddenly worried about what could possibly have the Council requesting their presence. Instantly, a wave of fear came over her. *The meeting! Had they somehow found out?*

Liotha's mind raced, her heart beating faster. The byway came into view, and within less than a minute they were joining the crowd gathered there, shifting into their true forms, and racing off toward the Central Sector and the Gates of Iteria.

It didn't take long for the gate to come into view, Liotha spotting the landing platform just outside the walls. She saw the Skyguard circling above. It seemed more than usual soared the sky at the moment. Another ill omen.

They landed hastily on the platform, quickly shifting and heading for the main gate. The guards there eyed them as they approached, joining several others in line. When they reached the front, Hel'aren showed them some papers proving right of passage for the two of them. The guards scrutinized the papers, eyeing Liotha warily. She tried to hide the look of guilt on her face, felt their eyes boring into her as she turned away. Finally, they nodded, handing back the papers and ushering the two of them through the gate.

Once inside, it was only a short walk to the Tempus of Fire – the High Council's domicile, where all matters of the dragon kingdom were discussed and decided upon. It was quite the spectacle. Liotha had admired it from the outside many times. This was to be her first inside. She wished it was under different pretenses.

The building itself was taller than most around it, other than the palace itself, which could be seen in the distance beyond the Tempus. Both were constructed mostly of Dragonstone–a dense, red rock that appeared crystalline in nature. The red stone was contrasted by the banners of the thirteen Scions–the leaders of the thirteen main families in dragon society. Liotha scanned them and located the banner for the Scion of Shaetalis, Mother Ere'daina's crest. A hint of hope shone amidst her fear. Perhaps Mother Ere'daina would be there to help, if the topic of debate was as she feared.

Hel'aren grabbed her wrist again and pulled her along, as she'd slowed to take everything in. Liotha snapped out of her thoughts and looked toward the entrance, noticing a large group gathered outside, everyone trying to see through the doors as guards barred entry.

Hel'aren pushed through the outer part of the crowd, still holding Liotha's wrist, making their way to the line of guards up front.

One of the guards, an exceptionally large one, even in his human form, held his hand out as Hel'aren and Liotha approached. He wore a sigil on his chest. Liotha wasn't quite sure, but she thought it indicated the rank of Drae'Vor, which placed him several ranks above her mate.

"Private entrance by request only," the wyrm noted in a deep tone.

"We have..." Hel'aren replied, trying to sound bold, "...been requested, that is."

"Name?" the guard asked.

"Drae'tar Hel'aren of the Royal Guard. And this is my mate, Liotha. We were asked to come for the Council's meeting."

"Drae'tar, eh? Hel'aren? Don't know the name. Raetir," he huffed, turning to a wyrm nearby. "Do you have a Hel'aren and Liotha on the request?"

"Let me look, sir," the other guard replied, studying a parchment he was holding. "Yes, here they are. All clear."

"Heh," the Drae'Vor grunted. "Unlucky," he said with a smirk, eyeing them again before tilting his head toward the entrance and stepping aside. Hel'aren smiled briefly and gave a short bow before heading up the steps, dragging Liotha behind him.

"Good luck," the guard called out as they passed, giving Liotha a particularly nasty grin. Liotha gazed past him at the crowd and all the guards staring at them as they entered the large outer doors. She felt a knot turn in her stomach, causing a pain that shot up her chest, making her feel nauseous.

Inside, the foyer was abustle with a dozen or so official-looking dragons, all in human form and adorned with various silks and fancy trappings, each bearing the marks of their Scions. These were, most likely, stewards and attendants for the Councilors. All of them stared at Hel'aren and Liotha as they made their way toward the open Council chamber doors. As they passed, some of them leaned in closer together, whispering.

Liotha wanted to be annoyed by their mannerisms, but her own fate was more pressing, and she was doing all she could to hold back tears and vomit, her stomach a jumbled mess of anxiety and apprehension.

Inside, the Council chamber opened up into a large space, the tapestries of the thirteen Scions situated in even portions around the circular area. In similar fashion, the large, circular table sat in the very heart of the room, and the in-ward-facing chairs of the Scions sat respective to their sections of the chamber.

Liotha managed a quick glance around the room and those who already in-habited it. Her attention was quickly drawn to the section of Scion Shaetalis, and to Mother Ere'daina, who sat in her chair in front of the banner. They exchanged a brief glance, but the elder dragoness seemed to pay her little heed before turning her head toward the center of the tables where a lone dragon stood.

He was adorned in regal attire–a long shirt with two tails, colored in shades of red and white matching his flowing trousers, held in place by an ornate golden buckle in the shape of a circular ring of metallic fire. He wore nearly knee-high leather boots and matching leather gauntlets, and upon his head sat a crown of golden metal interwoven with some of the most exquisite dragonstones Liotha had ever seen.

If she didn't feel so terrible, it would have been quite the exhilarating turn of events. But considering who it was standing before her, it only made matters worse.

Liotha had heard tales of Dro'Kal's regality and air, and of how he was quite the specimen to behold, both in his true form and his human body. His appearance now was befitting the rumors. But seeing him standing there, staring at them as they approached, his piercing blue eyes seemingly burning right through her frail exterior, Liotha felt quite the opposite.

As they drew closer, Liotha saw something else—something deeper beneath Dro'Kal's skin. His veins were showing more than what should be normal, and his eyes had a hint of madness in them. But it was more than that. His skin looked strange, almost as if it had a purple undertone to it.

"Ah, the last of our guests are here," Dro'Kal breathed, his words calm, yet threatening, snapping Liotha out of her stare. "Please, come closer and join your friends. Your name, drake?" he asked, directed at Hel'aren.

"It's Hel'aren, your Majesty—Drae'tar Hel'aren."

"Ah, Hel'aren. I've heard that name recently. Mostly good things. Let us hope this proceeding will not put a mark on that record…"

Dro'Kal smirked at Hel'aren and Liotha before turning to address the audience in the chamber.

"I'm sure you all are wondering why you've been invited here today," he started, looking over those standing beside Liotha and her mate.

She presumed they were the others who'd been summoned. She glanced down the line, scanning for Kel'ana. There was no sign of her and Liotha sighed, but she noticed several of the dragonesses amongst them had been in attendance in the preceding night's meeting. She held in a gasp, quickly turning her eyes back to Dro'Kal, then to Mother Ere'daina. Ere'daina noticed, returning Liotha's gaze with a stern look, gently shaking her head.

"There have been rumors of late that there are some who are… unhappy with my rule," Dro'Kal continued, eyeing the attendees. "Of course, there are always those who are unhappy with things. I'm sure at least half the Southern District would kill me in an instant if they had the chance, amusing though that would be. That is not, however, what I am referring to."

Dro'Kal paced around the circle of the table where the Councilmembers sat, now eyeing them as well, making his way around and toward the other end of the line opposite Liotha.

"These rumors speak of nobles even." Several gasps emanated from the line. "Nobles who've earned their stations and been given the right to live within the safety of the northern districts."

Dro'Kal eyed the group as he paced down the line. Liotha watched the expressions on several of the other dragons as they began to realize the true plight of their current predicament.

"This is an erosion of trust. I expect this sort of behavior from the commoners, but not... from you. Now I know," he said, holding up his hand as he walked toward the center of the room, silencing several objections, "some of you are thinking you have no reason to be here. You have no idea what I'm talking about. You are wondering why you, specifically, have been summoned."

Dro'Kal turned back toward the group and smiled a menacing smile, tilting his head sideways as he eyed them all.

"At least one member of each family here today was observed leaving the Southern District yesterday evening around the time of the report we received that a group of these... *rebels* was having a secret meeting."

A murmur spread through the group, gasps of disbelief, several cries from the dragonesses in attendance. Liotha's eyes grew wide as Hel'aren turned to her in dismay before calling out his own innocence.

The noises all around her began to drown together in a muffled roar. Thoughts raced through her head, her heart pounding. She began to feel nauseous again.

Dro'Kal held up his hand to silence their cries, but some continued.

"Silence!" he shouted, his voice booming with a surge of energy as his eyes flared brighter, a hint of the dragon inside formulating across his features. He clenched his jaw, seeming to hold it back. The noise of objections came to a halt, the echoes from Dro'Kal's shout slowly fading with it.

Dro'Kal smiled again, irritation apparent in his pursed lips and twitching face muscles.

"Though it may be that some of you are innocent, we must take certain precautions. These are grave accusations and must be met with swift reprimand. I wanted to have you all individually interrogated," Dro'Kal said, pausing to watch the looks of horror appear on many faces, including Liotha's. "However, I have been advised by my Councilors that an alternative route might prove more effective. As such, only those whose guilt has been proven need to pay the price."

Dro'Kal approached the group again, looking them all over with a sinister smirk. He seemed to delight in torturing them with his indirectness.

"We received an anonymous tip that a specific drake and his mate were spreading word of this rebellion amongst the nobles. We followed this lead and uncovered the truth, rooting out two of the conspirators. Drae'Vor Ma'talis," Dro'Kal called out. "Bring out the traitors."

The room grew silent, all eyes following the Drae'Vor as he motioned toward one of the side doors. Several moments later, two guards emerged from the shadows, behind them the outlines of two individuals.

Liotha strained to see who it was. She was at the end of the line opposite the entrance, and everyone kept stepping out in front of her to see. Gasps arose, along with a few stifled cries. Liotha stepped out further as the guards and the two prisoners approached the edge of the Council tables.

"Is that..." Hel'aren started, his mouth and eyes wide.

Liotha's heart stopped when she saw their faces. It was Kel'ana and her mate!

She placed her hand over her mouth, trying to stifle her own cry as her eyes started to swell. She looked again toward Mother Ere'daina in a begging manner, but the Mother only shook her head and gave Liotha a look that told her she needed to contain herself. Liotha bit her lip, trying to hold back the tide of distraught welling inside her. Liotha's eyes returned to her friend.

As they entered the center of the room, coming up beside Dro'Kal, Kel'ana's eyes met Liotha's. Kel'ana tried to look brave in the face of it all, but when their eyes locked, Liotha saw the anguish buried deep within.

"Now, now," Dro'Kal began, leaning closer to Kel'ana. "Don't look so sad. Because of you, your friends will go free. They should thank you really," he finished, turning and casting a pointed look at the group, his eyes finally resting on Liotha and lingering for a second longer than the rest.

"Because of your sacrifice, they shall live," he said with another grin, waving his arm toward the group. "Though I expect it may weigh considerably on their conscience. In fact, I'm hoping it does."

Standing up straight, Dro'Kal looked around at all who were gathered in the chamber.

"With the High Council as my witness, I, Dro'Kal, Lord of the Dragon Realms, Custodian of the Lands Beyond," he shouted, his eye twitching as he spoke the last title. "I hereby sentence these traitors, for conspiring against the Dragon Throne, and planning to murder its rightful ruler... to death."

A murmur of disbelief made its way through the group around Liotha as she stared at the scene before her. How could she let this happen? She was just as guilty as Kel'ana. She wanted to do something, but what could she do? Liotha tried to swallow, but her mouth was so dry it hurt.

"For a sentence such as this, every Councilmember must give their approval," Dro'Kal stated.

As Liotha's thoughts raced, Dro'Kal walked around behind Kel'ana and her mate, nodding to the Councilmembers one by one. Liotha watched as each nodded back, a sign of their approval. When Dro'Kal got to Mother Ere'daina, Liotha held her breath, hoping for one last saving grace. Ere'daina turned her head, looking over the group, her eyes landing on Liotha for a brief second before she looked back to Dro'Kal, and nodded.

Liotha's heart sank. There was no hope, the last few councilors giving their final nods of approval.

Dro'Kal smiled and turned back toward Kel'ana and her mate. In a blur, he reached up, faster than anyone could realize what was happening, his human hands shifting into a more draconic appearance as his claws extended. Kel'ana and her mate both made a slight grunt as Dro'Kal's claws pressed deep into their backs, his eyes flaring brighter and more sinister as their own began to flicker.

Kel'ana kept her gaze locked with Liotha's the whole time, her eyes widening as blood began to drip from the corners of her mouth. She held the look as long as she could until at last the light faded from her eyes, a single tear emerging and falling down her cheek. Just as she'd always been, Kel'ana was strong to the very end.

Liotha wrested her gaze away from the scene, tears finally welling in her eyes she could no longer hold back. She thought she heard the cries of several others, but she couldn't focus beyond her own grief, her legs feeling weak as she collapsed onto the floor.

Dro'Kal pulled his claws free, letting the bodies of Kel'ana and her mate slump onto the ground into the blood already pooling beneath their feet. He looked maniacal, almost blood-crazed, as if he'd truly relished in the killing. His veins continued to bulge, the purple coloration in his skin seeming to swirl before he finally got it under control and managed to return to his prior appearance.

He held out his bloody hand, beckoning to one of the nearby guards. The guard hastily approached and brought a rag, which Dro'Kal took and wiped away the blood. As he did, he turned his eyes back toward the group, smiling as he saw the anguish his actions had caused.

"Their crime was against me. It was fitting that I be the one to carry out the sentence. Now, as for you all. If I hear any more talk of rebellion, and any of your names are mentioned, you will ALL meet this same fate. Is that understood?"

Everyone stared at Dro'Kal as he spoke, unsure of exactly how to respond, many still in horror at what had just unfolded. Several nodded hurriedly, others looked back at the corpses of Kel'ana and her mate.

"I said, is that understood?" Dro'Kal boomed, his features shifting slightly again.

More nods ensued from everyone except Liotha, who slowly turned her head up and looked at him through tear-filled eyes. Dro'Kal noticed and held her gaze for a moment, unblinking, before finally smiling as he tilted his head and looked over everyone again.

"Good. Then, you are free to go."

No one moved for several seconds.

"Leave, before I change my mind!" Dro'Kal shouted.

That got everyone moving; everyone, except Liotha, who sat on her knees on the floor, staring at the body of her friend. Hel'aren grabbed Liotha's arm, trying to pull her up to follow the others out.

Dro'Kal turned and moved to the guards, speaking with them while everyone was leaving. After a brief word, he turned, seeing their eyes watching Liotha as she fought Hel'aren, not wanting to get up off the ground. Mother Ere'daina stopped and watched as well, along with the other council members.

"Unless you want to end up like them, I suggest you get your mate out of here, Drae'tar," Dro'Kal said, his voice cold.

"Let's go, Liotha," Hel'aren whispered loudly as he heaved her up onto her feet. "You're going to get both of us killed."

Liotha turned her eyes slowly toward him, hoping for some sympathy but his eyes were just as cold as Dro'Kal's tone. She would find no sympathy. She looked back at Kel'ana as Hel'aren pulled her arm, barely getting her to her feet.

As they exited the main door of the chamber, Liotha's eyes moved back to Dro'Kal. He was watching them leave with a sly smirk. Liotha held her gaze with his until the doors finally closed behind them.

Monster.

***

Liotha could scarcely remember how she got home. Everything was a blur as the image of Kel'ana's lifeless eyes filled her head. As they entered the house, her thoughts still clouded, she felt herself being slammed against one of the walls.

Snapping out of her trance, she stared into her mate's rage-filled eyes, his breath heavy as it brushed against her.

"This is all your fault. You were with her last night! Were you at that meeting?" Hel'aren yelled.

The shock of everything left Liotha speechless, and her mouth was so dry, she wasn't sure she could speak even if she wanted to.

"Well? Answer me!"

Liotha just looked at him as more tears filled her eyes.

"Gah!" Hel'aren exclaimed. "You're useless. Not sure I want to know, anyways. This is probably going to cost me my promotion, if they don't dismiss me outright! Damnit!" he shouted, slamming his fist against the wall next to Liotha's head. He stared at her for several seconds. Liotha saw a glimmer of the same madness she'd seen in Dro'Kal's eyes. It terrified her.

At last, he stepped back with a grunt and walked toward the couch. He stood there for a moment, not looking at her, his muscles twitching. With another outburst, he grabbed the couch and flipped it over with a crash, scattering items throughout the room. Liotha flinched against the wall. Hel'aren then turned and headed for the front door, stepping outside and slamming it behind him as he left, Liotha flinching again.

Now beside herself, she slid down the wall and slumped onto the floor in exhaustion. Her throat hurt. She desperately needed water, but she could scarcely move.

As she lay there on the floor, no more tears came. No more could come. Her breathing was heavy, and there was a pain in her stomach. She reached her hand down, resting it over where her future dwelt. The magic there felt less now. Her eyes wandered the floor in front of her, spotting the glass orb from her mother, its shattered remnants strewn about the room.

Liotha felt an exhaustion like she'd never known wash over her as the world slowly faded into darkness.

CHAPTER THREE

SCARS

Liotha opened her eyes, looking up at a ceiling that was not her own. For a moment, she did not move. She only lay there staring, her thoughts racing with a thousand visions–the death of her friend, Hel'aren's outburst, and blurred images of other things haunting her dreams, incoherent and shrouded in shadow. The smell of blood and death still lingered in her nostrils.

Liotha closed her eyes again. She was tired, so tired. She slowly began to finally feel her body, which ached with a pain she'd never felt before. Forcefully, she opened her eyes, moving her hands down to her stomach. She held her breath, freezing for a second in fear that her children were gone. But after several seconds, she began to sense them, though their presence was faint.

She sat up, fighting the stiffness in her muscles to get into a sitting position, her head throbbing as she did. She swallowed, looking around the room. She remembered the thirst that had caused her to faint.

I don't feel as parched. Did someone give me water?

Liotha examined her surroundings. It was devoid of any décor other than the bed she was laying on and a nightstand next to it where an oil lantern sat burning, its dull light casting an eerie glow across the walls of the strange place. She forced her legs over the side of the bed and gently touched her exposed toes to the floor, a cool sensation seeping into her feet. It felt good against her skin, which currently felt like it was burning.

Realizing she was hot, she felt her forehead, sweat sticking to her hand. Glancing upward, she saw the door of the room had been left open. There was a dim glow emanating from the hallway. Liotha pressed her feet fully against the floor and stood, using her hand to hold the bedpost to steady herself as a rush of blood came to her head. She waited for a moment until it passed, finally standing all the way up.

Her legs felt weak, but she was able to stand on her own. Carefully, she lifted one foot and stepped forward. Her balance felt off, and she steadied herself before moving the next foot. Several more careful footfalls and she was through the door and out into a narrow corridor looking like it led out into a larger room up ahead.

She kept walking toward it, reaching out her fingers and running them along the walls on either side. They felt cool, too.

Stepping out into the larger room, a breeze swept across her skin, coming from an open balcony to her left. Liotha stood there for a moment, closing her eyes and relishing in the cool wind as it caressed her damp skin.

"About time you woke…" came a voice from the shadows to her right.

Liotha spun, watching a figure emerge, a dragoness in her human skin, dark with eyes a piercing green. Her hair was tied in tightly woven rows on either side of her head, the rest flowing freely above, curled spirals that came down toward her forehead. She wore a tight-fitting set of polished armor, painted in various shades of green and turquoise. Her face was expressionless as she stared at Liotha, who finally realized she was staring awkwardly back. She should have been startled, but the aching in her body and the throbbing of her head still dulled her mind.

"Where am I?" Liotha asked weakly.

"Somewhere safe. Come," the stranger replied, turning and heading toward a set of stairs that led up and away from the balcony.

Liotha waited for a moment, beginning to contemplate her situation. *They nursed me back to health. There should be nothing to fear, right?* Still, she had no idea who this dragoness was and why they'd brought her to this unknown place.

"Well, come on. Mother Ere'daina is waiting."

Mother Ere'daina? More questions raced through her head.

Liotha scrunched her brow, a hint of anger forming on her face as she remembered how Ere'daina had nodded her approval, resulting in Kel'ana's death. She followed the strange dragoness, ascending the stairs at a quicker pace, though every step felt like fire burning in her muscles.

The armored dragoness led Liotha up the stairs and through several hallways, never saying a word.

"Was it… *you* who nursed me back to health?" Liotha asked, breaking the awkward silence.

"Not me. I just brought you here."

"Oh, I see. Well, thank you…"

"Taura."

"Excuse me?"

"My name. It's Taura," the dragoness said, cocking her head sideways.

"Oh, right. Thanks, Taura."

Taura merely grunted with a slight nod of her head, picking up her pace and making for the large doorway at the end of the hall. Liotha saw more light ahead and began to feel another breeze.

She shielded her eyes as they emerged out onto a large balcony, the sun blinding her for several seconds until her eyes adjusted. As they did, she saw they were high above Dor'Dragos, somewhere along the side of Mount Dicendia—the massive volcano, from which the rivers of lava descended and powered the great dragon machines of the Western Sector.

As Liotha scanned her surroundings, her eyes met a familiar sight on the far side of the open area. Mother Ere'daina was standing a dozen feet to her left along the balcony's edge, gazing out over the city.

"It's beautiful, isn't it?" Ere'daina asked, not looking in Liotha's direction.

"I suppose," Liotha replied, staring at it a moment. But in truth, it seemed... less than it had before. Turning back toward Ere'daina, she took several quick steps forward.

Taura stepped in front of her, reaching out her arm to slow Liotha's approach. Ere'daina held up her hand, waving Taura aside as she looked at Liotha.

"It's quite alright, Taura. Liotha is a friend. Come, child," she said, motioning with her hand for Liotha to approach.

Liotha looked at Taura, who eyed her warily, then glanced down at the blade attached to Taura's hip.

"Taura, would you stop threatening the poor girl. She's already been through enough."

Liotha cast an awkward smile at Taura, then moved closer to join Ere'daina at the balcony's railing.

"How are you feeling, my dear?" Ere'daina asked.

"I'm alive, thanks to you two it seems," she answered, looking briefly in Taura's direction. "But Kel'ana... she's not, and that's also thanks to you." Liotha finished, a hint of anger in her voice. She sensed Taura tense up off to the side.

"I understand your frustration. It was—"

"Frustration? My best friend is dead, and you did nothing to stop it! I'm more than frustrated!" Liotha burst out in anger, tears beginning to well in her eyes.

Taura took several steps closer, putting her hand on her blade. Ere'daina shot her a glance and shook her head.

"I'm... I'm..." Liotha couldn't complete her words, tears escaping as she leaned against the railing, using it to help keep herself from crumbling over as a fresh wave of emotions washed over her.

Mother Ere'daina stepped closer, placing her hand on Liotha's shoulder. Liotha shrugged away momentarily, her tears causing small splatters on the railing. After waiting a moment, Ere'daina moved toward her again, placing her hand on Liotha's shoulder.

"I'm so sorry, Liotha. I, too, grieve Kel'ana's loss. She was a dear friend."

Liotha's crying slowed and she sniffled, trying to collect herself. Slowly, she looked up toward the older woman, who was smiling warmly at her.

"Why then? Why didn't you stop it?"

Ere'daina's expression turned to sorrow, her eyes moving away from Liotha as she paused a moment.

"It was the only way. If Dro'Kal didn't have his vengeance, then I fear he would have uncovered the rest of you. And if that happened, we would be grieving you and the others as well right now."

"I could have resisted their questioning," Liotha replied.

"Perhaps, but the Wyrmlord's inquisitors are ruthless. Many have died from their questioning. Someone would have broken, and then we'd all be in danger of discovery. It was better one died in order to save the many."

"Two," Liotha corrected her.

"Yes—I mean, two. Kel'ana and Yoras were valuable assets to our cause. Their presence will be missed."

"Assets? Is that all she was to you?"

"No, of course not. I— I only meant she was a big help and proponent of what we are trying to do. She was a beautiful dragoness, of course. I'd known her for some time and grown quite fond of her. She brought many to our cause. She brought you, after all," Mother Ere'daina finished with a smile.

Liotha looked into her eyes, as if searching for the sincerity behind the words. Somewhat satisfied by what she saw, she shifted her demeanor, shooting another quick glance at Taura as she wiped more tears from her face in shame.

"I want nothing to do with your rebellion," Liotha said with a renewed energy. "It took my friend from me, and it almost took me too. I will not support the deaths of more innocents."

Ere'daina stared at her for a moment. Liotha could not comprehend what was happening behind the elder dragon's exterior. Mother Ere'daina turned back toward the city and placed her hands on the railing, taking in a deep breath and letting it out slowly.

"I have lived within these walls my entire life, nearly 800 cycles now. I have seen three Wyrmlords sit upon the throne. Their thirst for power has always been apparent, and the inhabitants of this city have paid for their greed. Growing up in the *Sentina*, I saw it more than most of the nobles up here," she continued, taking note of Liotha's questioning look at the mention of the term the nobles used for the worst part of the Southern District. "Yes, I was born a commoner. Escaping the clutches of the *Sentina* was no easy feat, but that is a story for another time. During my time there, I saw many die due to starvation and disease, all due to the Throne's lack of support. And because of this, the dragons of the Southern District often turned on each other, simply to survive. Many died merely because they wished to make a better life for themselves. Some even tried to sneak into the northern districts. It never ended well. I worked my way up the right way because I thought like they did—I thought it would be better. But shortly after I'd settled in the Western District, that's when I met Zareena."

Mother Ere'daina's eyes met Liotha's, whose eyes widened in remembrance of the name. A pained smile formed on Ere'daina's face before she continued.

"That's when I learned that monsters come in all forms. It wasn't just the lowlifes and miscreants. It went all the way to the top."

Ere'daina paused again, a pained expression etched in the lines of age across her face.

"Some things never change, my dear. But these last fifty cycles of living under Dro'Kal's rule has extended beyond anything I've seen before. His predecessors were cruel and apathetic, but they did not dare upset the balance of the world.

Dro'Kal is different. His greed extends beyond mere wealth and rule over the kingdoms. He desires something much more. As I told everyone at the meeting, he has been consuming the fonts of power throughout the world for some time now. What I didn't say was how many. I didn't want to scare everyone, but it's much worse than I let on. The other races are dying, barely able to survive with their flows of magic cut off. Some have already moved their people underground in an effort to find access to the leylines. I do not know if it will be enough. If they don't find enough magic..." Ere'daina stopped, giving Liotha a sorrowful look.

"The world is dying, Liotha. If we don't stop him, I fear it will be the end of us all. You saw him at the summoning. I know you saw it."

"There was something... off about him, yes," Liotha replied. "But if what you say is true, then how can we hope to stop him. Isn't he too strong already?"

"Maybe," Ere'daina sighed. "But that's why we need to hurry. That's why we need everyone we can get. That's why we need *you*."

"Why me? What am I against... *him*? How can one *saureen* possibly make a difference?"

"You're much more than you know, Liotha," Mother Ere'daina smiled as her eyes gazed deep into her own.

"I..." Liotha started, turning away from Ere'daina's gaze, her cheeks turning pink. "I don't feel strong. Everything hurts, and I just want to go home and rest. My mate will be upset if I'm gone too long. I must do what I can to keep my children safe," she finished, placing her hands on her belly.

Ere'daina smiled, but there was an apparent despair behind it Liotha could not ignore. Ere'daina glanced down at Liotha's belly.

"I understand this is a lot to ask of you. You don't need to give me your answer right away. Go. Rest and heal some more while you think on it. Just be careful—and hurry. We don't have much time."

"I'll... think on it," Liotha offered. *No, I won't.*

"Very well. Taura can show you the way out."

Liotha looked at Taura and nodded, then turned back to Ere'daina.

"Thank you for your help," Liotha said with a bow, hesitating a moment. Her thoughts drifted to Hel'aren and his fit of rage. She hoped it was merely a harsh overreaction to the stress of everything. She was sure he'd have calmed down by now.

Mother Ere'daina nodded in reply, then turned back to the balcony's edge to gaze out over the city again. Liotha let her thoughts go and turned to follow Taura, who was already at the hallway entrance, beckoning Liotha to follow. Liotha took several steps, paused and looked back toward Mother Ere'daina one last time. She wanted to say more, but after several seconds, her face twitched and she turned away, following Taura into the dark tunnel.

***

As Liotha landed in the Northern District's byway and transformed back into her human skin, she felt a sudden sense of being out of place, as if everything around her was foreign now. She tried to shrug it off, but it nagged at her as she walked cautiously toward her home, keeping her head down, her cheeks red in shame and fear lest anyone she recognized spot her. She walked past several others, strange glances cast her way. She thought she heard whispers. *Do they somehow know?*

When she arrived home, the door to the house was closed, but she could see the splinters in the wood from when Hel'aren had slammed it. It creaked as she opened it, the sound causing her heart to flutter. It was completely quiet inside, the place still a mess from when she was last there.

Did Hel'aren ever come back?

She wandered carefully through the wreckage of the room, examining the damage fully now. Her eyes were immediately drawn to the glass shards of her orb. A sadness overtook her as she knelt down and started picking them up, tears welling in her eyes, though she held them back and swallowed.

Hel'aren was just angry. I'm sure everything will be fine.

She finished picking up the fragments of the orb, including the smashed pieces of her egg. She held them up, examining them sorrowfully. Memories of when her mother first gave it to her filled her mind. She still felt like crying, but for some reason, her feelings had calmed, a strange dullness replacing them. Perhaps, she just kept running out of tears.

Liotha carefully took the shards of the orb and headed for her room, placing them gently on her nightstand, rummaging through her clothes for something to wrap them in for protection until she could attempt to get the orb repaired. She found one of her winter scarves and brought it over, gently placing the broken glass and eggshells on it, wrapping it up and tying a knot to keep them from falling out. Placing it under her bed, she stood back up and looked out through the doorway at the mess in the main room. With a sigh, she headed toward it to get to work.

A short time after getting started, Liotha paused, taking a glance outside to see the hour was growing late. As she waited, she began to hear heavy footsteps outside. Her ears pricked at the sound, her heart pounding louder in her chest. Several seconds later, Hel'aren burst through the door with a scowl on his face.

"Where the bloody hell have you been!?" he asked, his eyes wide and filled with anger when he spotted her.

"I was–"

"Were you out at another meeting? Did you not learn your lesson the first time?" Hel'aren accused, stepping toward her.

"No, I wasn't. I was just–"

"Do you really expect me to believe that?" Hel'aren said as he continued walking toward her in a menacing manner. "Where else would you have been?"

"I was hurt. You–"

"You were hurt? I'm the one who's paying the price for your carelessness. I was told there was little chance I'd be considered this Selection, thanks to you and

Kel'ana. The only way for me to have any chance at all is a divine act to prove my loyalty."

"Is that all you care about? Your promotion! Kel'ana is *dead*," Liotha shot back, a sudden vein of courage welling inside her.

"She's dead because she was a traitor. That has nothing to do with me. You know how hard I've worked for this, and yet you don't see a problem colluding with traitors who want to see the Wyrmlord removed from the throne. It's you who should feel ashamed, not me."

Hel'aren had drawn near to Liotha now. She saw the difference in his eyes, the way his skin tensed, almost crawling, the dragon within squirming to break free. She could hear his heart pounding faster, his anger growing. She took several steps backwards, fearful he was going to strike her again.

"In fact, perhaps divine retribution has been staring me in the face this whole time. You deserve to be punished. And perhaps if I'm the one to do it..." Hel'aren premised, looking at Liotha with a new perversion in his eyes.

Hel'aren stepped forward and grabbed Liotha's wrist, pulling her toward him and grabbing her throat with his other hand. Releasing her wrist, he brought his other hand up and placed it on the left side of her face. Liotha tried to struggle but he gripped tighter on her throat. He began speaking the ancient draconic words of fire magic.

Ab intus si'vocan te'alis. Ignis fex viceren. Ignis fex animaeus.

Liotha's eyes grew wide as she heard the words. She'd studied enough magic to know what Hel'aren was attempting. If she was in her dragon form, the spell would do little against her scales. But in this skin, it could easily burn her flesh.

She tried to shift, but it only made his grip tighter. The air in her lungs began to grow thin.

Several moments later, she started to feel it. With each passing second, the heat from Hel'aren's hand intensified. She could feel the flesh on her face beginning to sear. He wasn't very adept at magic, and it was slow, but gradually getting hotter. She struggled against Hel'aren's grip, letting out a cry, the pain shooting through her body. But try as she might, his grip was too strong.

The heat continued, and by now, the pain was so intense she felt herself starting to lose consciousness.

Monsters come in all forms.

The words of Mother Ere'daina came to her. Liotha looked up with her free eye, staring into the eyes of the one she'd called *consori*. His eyes were not the same. He was not the same. He looked like–like Dro'Kal had looked. He looked like a monster.

You're much more than you know. Mother Ere'daina had seen something in her. Why couldn't she see it? What was stopping her?

Liotha's mind shifted to the story of Zareena, how she had accepted her fate and died a tragic death, all her potential lost due to the actions of a monster.

No...

Liotha's mind snapped back to the present, her eye focusing on Hel'aren. It began to glow brighter, casting a purple hue against Hel'aren's skin. She felt a surge of energy well within her. She didn't know where it came from, but she tapped into it and pulled, letting it explode out of her with a force so great she sent Hel'aren reeling backward, crashing over the furniture she'd just rearranged.

Without much control, Liotha continued to fume, immediately shifting into her true form, her wings spreading wide. As she grew, she exploded through the roof, pieces of their home scattered into the street, others slamming into nearby houses. She didn't care anymore. She scanned for her mate, eyeing Hel'aren hiding behind the crashed sofa. With a menacing growl in her belly, the heat rising within, she craned her neck backward. She meant to strike. She meant to end him.

Peering down at his horrified face, Liotha paused for just a moment, realizing what she was doing. *Am I the monster now? But this is justice, is it not?* She did not want to become the very thing she sought to destroy. *But... how then? How does one destroy a monster without losing their soul in the process?*

Liotha heard the sound of wings and came to, pushing her thoughts aside. She saw Hel'aren had escaped and took to his own dragon form, sailing into the sky, heading toward the Central District. Understanding the seriousness of her situation, Liotha stopped and transformed back into a human. She needed to get out of there quickly. Hel'aren would likely return with the guards in minutes.

Liotha ran to her room, stepping over the ruins of the now crumbled house and through the barely standing doorway. Her room hadn't been as damaged as the main living area, but there were still debris everywhere, chunks of wall having smashed into her bed, which was cracked in several places and sagging. She headed straight to her closet to look for something that would cover most of her body.

She saw a dark purple cloak in the back of her closet, which had been a gift from her mother when she was joined with Hel'aren. She'd never much liked it, as she'd always been ashamed of her purple eyes and how rare they were. But now, things were different. She grabbed the cloak and threw it over herself, stumbling out of the room and toward the front door. In her haste, she'd completely forgotten about the shards of the orb still hidden under the bed.

Out in the street, there were a dozen or so residents who'd come to investigate what was going on. Liotha blushed and pulled the hood of her cloak over her head. She took one last look at the house, a momentary sadness filling her heart. There had been so many hopes and dreams contained there. The dreams felt distant now, as if they belonged to someone else. She wondered how many of those dreams had truly been her own anyways.

Those dreams were chosen for me. My fate leads down a different path.

Liotha reached her hand down to her belly. She felt turmoil amongst the magic there, as if her children sensed her pain and sorrow and anger, as if they felt it with her. There were still some dreams that were her own, and she was bringing them with her.

I must protect you. I will protect you.

Liotha turned away from the crowd and ran down the street, disappearing into the darkness of the night, leaving behind the shattered fragments of her past, heading for the only place where she knew she'd be safe. Fate had forced her down a new path. Perhaps it was supposed to be with Mother Ere'daina all along.

CHAPTER FOUR

MONSTERS

W hen Liotha awoke, she looked up at the same ceiling she'd gazed upon only just the other day. Today, it was she who felt strange and unfamiliar.

The truth was, she'd been lying in that room staring at that ceiling for days, though how many, she knew not. Part of her hadn't had the strength to get up, part of her hadn't wanted to. She needed time to process everything that had happened. Though she wasn't sure she was ready, she needed to get up and distract herself with something.

She sat up, grunting through the sore muscles and tenderly touched her face, flinching in pain. The flesh had healed a little, Mother Ere'daina bringing in a healer to tend to the wound. She'd left her with some sort of balm to help with the healing process. It had helped a little, especially since it felt cool when applied, but the burns were deep, and Liotha had been told they might not ever fully heal.

It will serve as a constant reminder of my past failures.

Liotha stood up, her muscles still sore, but mostly healed by now. Fortunately, those wounds had been less severe, and her natural healing helped alleviate them quickly, unlike her face.

Entering the next room, Liotha rounded the corner and headed straight for the stairs. A figure emerged from a shadowed corner, causing Liotha to jump.

"Must you always slink through the shadows, Taura?" she huffed, catching her breath.

"I like the shadows. Better to see and listen as everyone spills their secrets."

"You're not going to get any secrets from me. I have nothing left to hide."

"Everyone has secrets. We'll just have to wait and see what yours are."

There was an awkward pause as Liotha and Taura exchanged wary glances. Finally, Taura relaxed slightly, changing the subject.

"You look like shit."

"Wow, thanks," Liotha replied with a frown, still too exhausted to really care at the moment. "How long was I in there?"

"It's been almost a week. With everything you went through, Mother thought it best to wait for you to emerge on your own."

Liotha nodded, her eyes distant and her thoughts drifting back into dark places.

"Sorry."

"Sorry what?" Liotha asked, snapping back to reality.

"That wasn't nice—what I said."

"What did you say?" Liotha asked, slightly confused.

"About you looking like shit. I suppose I would, too."

"Ah, that..."

"I've been told I tend to be a bit abrupt."

"A bit?" Liotha replied.

"A bit..." Taura countered, slightly more serious, though she gave a quick smirk. "Anyways. Ready to go see Mother?"

Liotha nodded. Taura wasted no time, ascending the same stairs, just as they'd done before. But this time, they headed right from the top, down several hallways, and then descended a much wider staircase that spiraled downward into a large open area. There was a fire flickering in the large stone hearth, some kind of white marble fashioned with gold edging, and an assortment of fancy chairs and a large sofa strewn about the floor in front of it. Above the fire hung a large picture of a dragoness, scales silver and eyes shining like brilliant amethysts.

Zareena...

To their left, on the opposite side of the room, Liotha could see into a large room that appeared to be surrounded on all sides by walls filled completely with books. There was a large table sitting squarely in the middle, several comfy-looking chairs sitting around it. It appeared to be some sort of study.

Taura continued to lead Liotha through the room and into another, this one a kitchen. It was neat and tidy, looking like it hadn't been used to prepare a meal in ages. Either it wasn't, or somebody was an excellent cleaner.

Past the kitchen, they made their way through another long hallway with several small side rooms until they came at last to what Liotha could only assume was just inside the main entrance to the building. She did not know for sure, as she'd only ever entered and exited through the landing pad on the roof—at least, when she'd come consciously.

"Ah, you're awake. Perfect," said Mother Ere'daina as she descended one of the curved stairs that descended from another level of the residence.

Liotha turned toward her and approached the foot of the stairs to greet her with a short bow.

"How are you, my dear?"

"I feel about as good as I look, I suppose," Liotha replied, her tone dulled. She stole a quick glance at Taura. It wasn't entirely false, but in all honesty, she didn't really know how she felt.

"Tsk, tsk. Let me have a look at you."

Mother Ere'daina reached out her hand and put it under Liotha's chin, turning her head from side to side as she eyed the scar from the burn.

"It could be worse, but it could be better, too. I can request the mender return for more sessions."

"Don't bother. I'm fine..."

"Are you sure? It's worth–"

"Yes. Let's just get to what's more important. We've wasted too much time, and given I've lost nearly everything," Liotha said, placing her hand down to her stomach, "I'm ready to help. Perhaps I can be of some use, after all."

Mother Ere'daina smiled, a slight twinkle in her eye.

"If you're up for it?"

"Yes, I'm ready. What do you need me to do?"

"Walk with me," Mother Ere'daina said with a pleased smile, turning and heading out the other side of the room, opposite where Liotha had entered.

Liotha followed, Taura beside her, as they made their way through the house and down more stairs. She marveled at the sheer scale of the abode. For all its size, it seemed to just house her and Taura–and perhaps, the occasional guest, such as Liotha, though she'd not seen anyone else so far and imagined that was probably normal.

Eventually, they came out onto a large balcony, which Liotha recognized immediately as the one where they'd met before.

"The execution of Kel'ana was a setback," Mother Ere'daina started, gazing out over the city. "Many of the other dragonesses are too afraid to even meet after what they saw. I don't blame them," she finished, looking at Liotha. "But things are getting worse, and we cannot afford to wait for them to come back around. That is where I hope you can help."

Liotha gave Mother Ere'daina an inquisitive look.

"I heard you graduated top of your class at Peritina. Your parents must have been proud."

"Hmph," Liotha scoffed. "Sure."

"Oh, come now. That's quite the achievement for a dragoness from Nu'haren. Even being accepted into Peritina is tough for dragonesses from the Scions. Yet you pulled it off, and you bested every single one of them to graduate with the highest honors. That takes a real resolve, and a sharp wit to go with it."

"Have you been spying on me?"

"Spying? Not exactly. But I do take the liberty to monitor the city for notable events, and potential future alliances. All the Scions do it, of course, but none of them are as good as me."

Taura cleared her throat.

"As we are," she corrected, smiling slyly at Taura. "So yes, I have had my eye on you for quite some time now."

"Well, if that's the case, then you'd know my parents only sent me here to get a proper education so I could prove a worthy mate for one of the Royals. Of course, even with my accolades, best I could do was a drake from one of the lesser Scions who was enlisting as a Drae'tar in the Royal Guard."

"Yes, I am sorry things didn't go as planned," Mother said. "But be that as it were, many of the other Scions wrote you off. I, however, knew better. Believe me when I say this, but this was not how I wanted you to come to aid our rebellion. I am, however, pleased you are here now," Mother Ere'daina turned, taking Liotha's hands.

"Didn't go as planned..." Liotha said, pulling her hands away slowly as she turned to look out over the city, pausing for a moment. "I never wanted to join with Hel'aren. I barely knew him, but arranged marriages are such the way out in Nu'haren. I was young and naïve. For all my intelligence, I was blind to the error of that course. How could I have not seen what he'd end up becoming?"

"Monsters aren't born, Liotha," Mother said, a distant look forming in her eyes. "They become such, slowly, over time, every wrong choice sending them down a darker path until, eventually, the shadows are all they know. The process may be slow, but in the final moments, it can happen in the blink of an eye. Sometimes we are blind to the shadows until night has become our new reality."

"I will never be so blind again. These scars won't let me forget," Liotha countered, feeling an anger welling up in her now.

"We both hold scars, though in different forms. We must not be afraid of them—must embrace them, even. It is what reminds us of what they are capable of."

"Yes, scars..." Liotha hesitated. "What point are you getting at by bringing all this up? What does my schooling have to do with the rebellion?"

"Yes, right. What I meant was that you have a sharp wit, and that's exactly what we need right now. We need something that will draw the others to our side—something that will prove to them how much of a monster Dro'Kal and his cohorts are. And we need something to show them we can defeat him."

"Right. And you think I can just come up with something overnight?"

"I am putting a great deal of faith in you, Liotha, yes, but I am not sending you on this task empty-handed. In my study, you will find an assortment of books and documents we've collected. They should be of great use to you. We've gathered every bit of intelligence we can on Dro'Kal, the palace, and his dealings in the shadows. I have also gathered an extensive collection of copies of the tomes on ancient magic, including some that many consider... objectionable."

The two dragonesses eyed each other, Liotha's eyes lighting up with intrigue.

"I thought that might spark your interest. I know you had a strong curiosity in magic during your studies, did you not?"

"Maybe," Liotha replied, tilting her head to the side with a shrug. "How did you get such tomes?"

"A Scion has many resources at her disposal," she replied with a smirk, her eyes dodging toward Taura. Liotha glanced her direction, Taura keeping mostly a straight face as her eyes moved to meet Liotha's temporarily. "No matter, they are at your disposal now. To destroy a monster, sometimes one must make... sacrifices. For the greater good, of course."

"For the greater good," Liotha said with an apathetic chuckle.

"Anyways, the whole of the study is at your disposal. I trust it will be enough to fuel your curiosity. Just make sure you focus on the task at hand. You can get started as soon as you are ready," Mother Ere'daina said as she started to walk off.

"Where are you going?" Liotha asked, a bit taken aback.

"Taura and I have work to do telling the others about our plan."

"I thought we didn't have one yet?" Liotha replied, clearly confused.

"We do. It's just in your head. So, get to work fleshing it out. Don't make me a liar, Liotha," Mother Ere'daina ended as she turned and ascended the stairs, leaving Liotha standing alone on the balcony in her confusion.

Liotha sighed and moved to the balcony's edge, standing in silent contemplation while she gazed out over the whole of Dor'Dragos. The city looked different now—more distant, and in some ways, even unfamiliar.

Is it even worth saving? Are they worth saving?

As if in response, she felt a gentle flutter from the magic within her belly. She placed her hand there. *At least some are worth saving, like you, my love.* Liotha forced a smile.

Perhaps, it was just she who was different now. Perhaps, it was she who needed saving the most. Liotha looked back up the steps where Mother Ere'daina had disappeared. A look of pained determination illuminated her features as she reached up to feel the scars on her face again.

A reminder. Mother believes in me. Maybe if I save the world, I can find my own redemption and sense of purpose along with it. Maybe.

Looking back over the city, Liotha nodded, acknowledging her own willingness to do what needed to be done to save not just them, but somehow, also herself. With an apprehensive heart, she turned and ascended the stairs, recalling the way to the study. She had a lot of work to do, and it was time to get started.

***

Liotha spent well into the night looking through the papers and books that had been strewn about the desk. For the first few hours, she read in intrigue about Dro'Kal—his comings and goings, those he consorted most closely with, the hourly schedules of the palace guard, and any other details that Mother had deemed of import to their plans. It had all been well and good, and there were many details about what Dro'Kal was up to that intrigued Liotha, but there were other interests that kept her skimming notes until she got to the first of several tomes Mother Ere'daina had acquired.

Though there were several, one in particular caught her eye. Liotha set it before her, admiring its frayed red leather binding, its surface still smooth to the touch, intricate black symbols and words in the ancient tongue carved onto its front and spine. It was clear the tome was exceptionally old. Liotha had learned the old script in her studies at Peritina, but it was difficult to read nonetheless, as it was impossible to account for the varied dialects that had surfaced during the First Age. In addition to that, many who studied the old magics weren't exactly known for their handwriting.

The cover, at least, had been etched by a master artist, and the lettering was clear as the day it was engraved. Liotha pulled on the strings of her thoughts, weaving the threads of memory together until the words on the cover came to her in the common tongue: "A Compilation of Transformational Magic".

This is objectionable, indeed. Delightful.

Liotha hastily opened the cover, though she took care as she could feel the binding was loose. The first few pages were introductory, providing the names and statuses of those who'd contributed to the tome's creation. Most of it was of little use to Liotha, but just before she was about to turn the page a name caught her eye–Aurelio Vesarian.

A human name? How could that be? Humans do not understand the ways of magic. It was rare indeed for humans and dragons to get along, much less work together. And yet one had seemingly worked with her ancestors producing this relic.

Liotha's face showed her deep confusion, but her curiosity to delve into the actual contents of the tome quickly overtook it.

The next few pages covered more background on the research, Liotha skimming those as well. Nothing of note popped out at her until she reached another couple pages further. There, as the title of the page, was the first listed magic. *Dicerevis*–the magic of altering another's thoughts.

"That would be useful," Liotha said out loud. Lifting her head, she looked around awkwardly but seeing that no one was around to hear her.

She continued reading, the tome talking about how to perform the ancient art of mind-control. It was a complicated magic, and seemingly only worked on those weak of will, or those whose minds had been weakened or distracted. It was something Liotha would certainly study, but not something that would likely help them against one as powerful as Dro'Kal.

Another couple pages and she came across one titled *acroturas*. It was the magic of projection, allowing one to create images to confuse or disorient. It was a neat trick, but Liotha wasn't sure there would be much application in their case. Dro'Kal would not be swayed by such cheap tricks.

She continued on, flipping through pages of magics she'd only ever heard rumors of, and others still she did not know were even possible. Despite many of them having their uses, such as *somb'ulatura*–or dream-walking–none of them seemed to be what the rebellion needed to succeed. Liotha needed something strong to subdue Dro'Kal.

Over the next few hours, she skimmed through dozens more tomes until her exhaustion finally overcame her.

***

Liotha stirred to the sound of knocking. Apparently, two straight days couped up in this study was more tiring than she would've expected.

She lifted her head from the desk, looking around in a state of confusion, her mind still numb from sleep. The knocking came again.

She faced the door, finally realizing someone was on the other side.

"Come in," she spoke up, though it wasn't as loud as she'd intended.

The door creaked open nonetheless and Taura appeared in the doorway holding something in her hands. As she drew closer to the desk, Liotha saw it seemed to be some sort of woven basket. Taura placed it on the desk in front of Liotha, who was still trying to rub the sleep out of her eyes. When Liotha saw the basket, a wooden lid covering the contents, she sat up straighter, then gazed up at Taura with a raised eyebrow.

"What's this?" Liotha asked.

"Well, open it," Taura replied.

Always straight to the point with her, Liotha mused. She gave Taura a frown, then carefully opened the lid.

"My clothes?"

"There wasn't much left. The place was quite a mess."

Liotha's thoughts were pulled back into the nightmarish events of that evening. Weariness overcame her, and she felt her heartbeat quicken.

"There's more..." Taura said, pointing toward the basket.

Liotha emerged from her thoughts, looking back down at it. She reached inside and grabbed the clothes, her finger grazing against something smooth. As she lifted the clothes out and set them aside, she peered into the shadows of the basket. The lighting in the room made it difficult to see. Reaching inside, she put her fingers around what felt like a glass orb. Instantly, she remembered the shards of her orb she'd hidden under her bed. But it had been shattered.

Carefully, she brought it out and held it up into the light. It *was* her orb, and it had been repaired. Bubbled lines converged and dissected across the entire surface. The shards of her egg rested safely inside. Liotha's brow furled, and she looked up at Taura.

"How did you–"

"We know a great many dragons with special talents," Taura said. "There is a letter from Mother, too. Is there anything else you need before I leave?"

Liotha continued to marvel at the orb, barely murmuring "no" before Taura turned and disappeared through the doorway. After another minute, realizing she was alone again, she remembered what Taura had said. She carefully set the orb aside on the pile of clothes and reached inside to find a small piece of paper. Holding it up, she read the words inscribed on it:

Broken, but not lost. All can be mended with the right craft. You hold all the pieces in your hand.

Liotha read the words again. *All can be mended. I do not think my heart will be so easily mended. But maybe there is a truth to her words. She survived her grief, after all.*

Liotha read the last line again. *You hold all the pieces...*

Liotha's eyes opened wide in sudden realization. *That's it!*

She set the paper aside and scanned the open books strewn about the desk. *Somb'ulatura. Dicerevis. Acroturas. Even prae'natalis–the blood magic.* Perhaps, individually, they would not provide the answer, but together?

"Taura!" Liotha shouted, not sure if the dragoness was still lurking close enough to hear. After several seconds, the familiar shadow emerged through the doorway.

"Needed something after all?" she asked with a smug smirk.

"Go tell Mother I think I might have figured out how to subdue Dro'Kal," Liotha said, her mind still racing with all the possibilities–and implications.

Taura's smirk twisted into a devilish smile, and with a nod, she vanished again.

This just might work, but we're going to need some help. She glanced through the books she'd read. There was one she'd cast aside, thinking little of it initially, but the tome naming the human Vesarian and his study of blood magic gave her a new idea. The book she was looking for discussed the impacted regions of Dro'Kal's excursions, and those leylines yet consumed by Dro'Kal. There had been something in there about a human band of warriors who'd developed a knack for killing dragons, which had caused some problems in the region in the past. It was detestable, but maybe just the tool they'd need to provide an adequate distraction.

Monsters fighting monsters. This just might work...

Chapter Five

PLANS

L iotha's stomach churned, a sharp pain shooting throughout her midsection. She coughed, droplets of blood splattering into the sink below. It had been slowly improving since the incident, which was why she hadn't told anyone. She looked up at herself in the mirror. *It's just a side-effect of the trauma. It will pass.*

She wiped her mouth clean, continuing to stare at the reflection of herself–a reflection she barely recognized, though it'd only been just over a week since the night everything had changed. A mask now covered half her face, hiding her scars–another gift from Mother.

Mother had given it to her just hours before. It had been crafted by one of the Firesmiths in her employ. It was made of pure *ignalium*, a metal forged in the fires of Mount Dicendia, considered one of the strongest and most beautiful of all the known metals. Liotha had never been gifted something of such value. The precious metal was normally only possessed by royalty and other extremely wealthy individuals. Liotha initially refused the gift, but quickly relinquished due to Mother Ere'daina's insistence. Though the mask itself brought attention, it was better than everyone seeing her disfigured face. However, Liotha still felt a bit uncomfortable wearing it.

She tore her gaze away from the mirror to the closed door behind her. On the other side, what was left of the uprising was gathering for another meeting. She wondered how many would be willing to brave the attention they now faced.

Mother Ere'daina had put the call out to the others as soon as she'd heard Liotha's plans. They had no time to waste and needed help to enact them. They'd schemed together long into the night while Taura did what she did best, spreading the word in the shadows and arranging a new secret meeting place. Since the prior location had been compromised, they'd improvised and found an old, abandoned warehouse on the outskirts of the Western District. Taura thought perhaps avoiding the southern district might be best for now. The guard likely wouldn't expect a meeting under their noses. Liotha wasn't so sure, but she had little say in the matter.

Liotha turned back to the mirror, another knot sending pain through her stomach. She was going to be the one to reveal their plans. She didn't like it, but Mother had insisted that it would carry more weight coming from Liotha herself. And if there was any chance of persuading the others to fight after all that had happened, they needed every edge they could get.

A knock came from the door, Taura's muffled voice telling her it was time.

Liotha stole one more glance in the mirror, reminding herself why she was here–why she was about to go out there and convince the others they somehow had a chance. Dro'Kal was the reason her best friend was dead. He was the reason her mate tried to kill her. He was the reason she would forever wear these scars on her face. He, and any other monsters who chose to side with him, would pay.

Retreating from her inner turmoil, Liotha turned and left the bathroom. Outside, she noticed only a few had arrived. Including the three of them, she counted seven.

"This is it?" Liotha said quietly, coming over and leaning in next to Mother and Taura.

"Seems so," Taura replied, glancing over at Mother.

"I had hoped for more, but this will have to do. Perhaps after they hear our plans, the whispers will spread. If not, I have... other ideas."

Liotha gave Mother a curious glance but quickly saw that whatever idea she had, she would not be sharing the details. Liotha had never been used to so much secrecy, but she'd come to understand that in the world of politics–in Mother Ere'daina's world–secrecy was one's greatest weapon. Revealing too much could cost you. It could get you stabbed in the back. Now that Liotha had become a part of this world, whether she liked it or not, she was beginning to understand. It's why Mother had told her not to reveal *all* their plans.

"Shall we then?" Liotha asked. Mother nodded, then stood.

"Thank you all for coming today," Mother began. "We understand you are all taking risks to be here, given... recent events." Mother gave Liotha a nod of recognition. "Kel'ana was a beautiful soul. Her presence will be deeply missed."

Her words garnered several nods and sympathetic smiles from the others before continuing.

"Since every minute we linger puts us more in danger, I will get straight to the point. Liotha here has decided to join our cause."

Liotha dipped her head and smiled, her exposed cheek showing her embarrassment as eyes turned her way, some of them lingering with questioning expressions.

"Liotha has helped us devise a plan to put an end to Dro'Kal's reign of tyranny. It is a sound plan, and we are almost certain it will work. But in order to achieve it, we will need more than the three of us. So, Liotha will share our plans with you, and then you will share these plans with the others in an effort to bolster our numbers. Is this acceptable?"

Several nods came from the group, one or two others eyeing Liotha hesitantly. One of them, a dragoness named Kalira whose name Liotha remembered from the first meeting, spoke up.

"This... *saureen*," she started, eyeing Liotha's belly, "has only just joined our cause. Some of us have been coming to your meetings for months. How do we know we can trust her? How do we know she's not the reason why Kel'ana and her mate were discovered?"

Liotha's flush of embarrassment quickly turned to anger. She stepped forward to defend herself, but a wave of Mother's hand cut her short.

"Liotha is one of us. She has been through a great deal, and I am willing to put the entirety of this rebellion in the palm of her hands without question. That is how much I trust her. If you trust me, then you trust her."

Kalira's eyes darted between Mother and Liotha, her face twisted in indecision.

"Perhaps you trust her, Mother, and that is good to hear, but how do we know she is committed to the cause? You are asking us to put a great deal of faith in one who hides her true self behind a mask."

Liotha stepped forward, reaching her hand up toward the mask.

"You don't have to, Liotha," Mother said.

"It's alright. They need to know who they are putting their faith in, and why."

Liotha continued to reach up until her fingers wrapped around the front of the mask. Carefully, she pulled it away from her face. She kept her eyes locked on Kalira until the mask was fully removed, bringing it down to her side. Several gasps emanated from the group, hands covering their mouths in reaction to her scars. Kalira's own eyes grew wide in shock.

"You want to know if I am committed?" Liotha asked, her eyes still locked with Kalira's. "Dro'Kal is a monster, and any who side with him are the same. One such monster did this to me. As long as I draw breath, I will see every last one of them burn."

Liotha paused, letting her words sink in. They shocked even her to hear them out loud. She felt like she should be ashamed to think such thoughts, but her heart was heavy, her mind clouded with a dark fog of anger and resentment. And despite their intensity, she meant them.

"Does that alleviate your doubt, Kalira?" Liotha asked. She no longer felt timid in the presence of the others. Somehow, revealing her scars had given her a boldness she had not expected.

"Yes, quite," Kalira replied, a hint of submission in her voice, which only further emboldened Liotha.

"Very good. Then, shall we continue, Mother?" Liotha said, putting her mask back into place. After a smile and a nod from Mother, Liotha continued.

"Even if the others return to our cause, we do not have the numbers for a direct assault on Dro'Kal. In order to stand a chance, we're going to need some help. As such, we must seek outside help."

"Outside help? Who would help us?" asked one of the dragonesses.

"We are working on that," Liotha replied, having expected the question. "It will remain a secret until we are ready, but we believe," she said, looking to Mother for assurance, "that our offer will not be so easily dismissed."

Mother Ere'daina nodded, a smile of approval for the others to see.

"Even with this outside aid, we will still need all the dragons we can on our side. But like I said before, we must take care who we recruit. We must be sure they can be trusted. That is where you all come in. We need you to talk to our sisters. We understand many of them are scared. They had good reasons for not showing tonight. If we can restore their faith, they can still be assets to this cause. But if their willingness has been broken, then do not speak to them of our plans. Each of you must carefully assess these sisters, and any others, to see who we can trust. And we must do it quickly. Is that clear?"

"So, that's it? That's the entirety of our plans?" Kalira questioned, her eyes narrowed.

"That's as much as we're revealing at the moment, but there is... *one* more thing we need to address. Do any of you have much skill in the arcane? Any who've received formal training, that is."

Liotha watched the dragoness's faces as she finished her words. They looked back and forth between each other, expressions of curiosity and confusion apparent in their features. After several moments, Kalira spoke up again.

"I have had some tutelage in the arts," she said, eyeing the others. "But what exactly are you looking for?"

"Considering the danger we are all in," Mother interjected, eyeing Liotha, "that will be kept confidential and only told to those we choose for this task. We hope you understand. Whoever has had such training, we ask you to please stay behind so we might question you further about it. The others are free to go and begin the task Liotha has presented to you. We know that just being here has put you all in danger. We do not want to keep you any longer than necessary."

Blank stares permeated the room, followed by awkward glances before several dragonesses stood and retreated. Eventually, all but two stood–Kalira and one other, a slender dragoness with long black hair tied neatly in a bun behind her head. Though small in stature, it was clear there was a fierceness behind her jade-green eyes.

"Thank you for staying, Kalira, Hiroma," Mother Ere'daina said once the others had gone. "Liotha..." she finished, nodding.

"Yes, so, please briefly explain what training you have had and a little about your particular talents."

Kalira glanced over at Hiroma, waving her hand forward. Hiroma bowed her head, then looked over at Liotha and Mother as she began.

"I studied under my mother," Hiroma began. "She serves as *Malifica* to Scion Shar'ona. As such, she's taught me the ways of the craft, in hopes that I would one day follow in her footsteps. I am fluent in all forms of protection magic, in addition to detection and deception."

"Valuable skills, Hiroma. Thank you," Liotha said. "And Kalira?"

Hiroma bowed, sitting back in her seat as Kalira leaned forward.

"I studied under Arcanist Zamora, my aunt. As Primus of the Artifectorium, she is in charge of overseeing imbuements and restoration of magical artifacts. As such, I have learned how to transfer and convert power from one object to another. And, if necessary, to transfer power between forms and even elements."

Liotha's eyebrows raised. *These two are exactly what we need.*

She glanced over at Mother, her lips curled in a sly smile. Mother's eyes moved sideways from Liotha's direction and nodded to Kalira, who relaxed back in her seat. Liotha smirked, turning her attention back to the two sitting before them.

"Well, it seems you both have quite the unique skillsets. In fact," she said, glancing over at Mother again, "you have exactly the kind of skills we need. If you're willing, they are skills we can put to good use. But before you make your decision, know that ours will be the most important, and dangerous, task. Do not accept unless you are willing to put your lives at risk. We understand if you need a night to think it over."

Hiroma and Kalira eyed each other, hints of doubt in their eyes. Kalira turned her attention to Mother with a look that portrayed her hesitation.

"What Liotha says is true," Mother Ere'daina said, as if in reply. "What we're planning to do has never been done before. Even if we succeed in subduing Dro'Kal, we don't know if the rest of our plan will be possible. To succeed, we will have to push ourselves to the very brink of each of our capabilities. And we all understand the potential consequences if we do that. It is a serious risk you must consider."

More worried glances were exchanged between the two dragonesses before they both eyed Mother and Liotha for a few quiet seconds. Finally, Kalira stood, a look of determination in her eyes.

"Though my life may be in peril, I will gladly do it if it means the end of that monster. I do, however, have one question of Liotha."

Liotha raised an eyebrow to Kalira.

"What is your question?" she asked.

"Mother said this plan will be difficult, may not even be possible. It's your plan, is it not? Do you truly believe it can work?"

"I..." Liotha paused, unable to answer. She wasn't sure. The plan was crazy, and like Mother had said, it'd never been done before.

Feeling Mother's eyes boring into her, she turned and peered into her piercing eyes.

You may not be sure, Liotha, Mother's voice came into her head. *But I believe in you. You have a gift, and if you convince them to help you–* Liotha glanced over at Kalira and Hiroma, apprehensively awaiting her reply. *If they help you, you will succeed. Doubt yourself, and they will see it. Believe, and you will see what is truly possible.*

Liotha focused her attention back on Kalira.

"I... do," she said, her voice quivering ever so slightly. "I do," she said again with more surety. "It's bold, and as Mother said, it's never been attempted before. And it is dangerous, yes, but with all our skills combined, not impossible."

Kalira stared into Liotha's eyes for what felt like a dozen seconds, as if she were deciphering the surety behind Liotha's words. Liotha tried to seem resolute, hoping Kalira could not see the hints of doubt still lingering in her mind.

"Very well," Kalira said at last, relaxing her stance. "I am willing to see it through. Hiroma? Want to help us end this bastard?" Kalira said, extending her hand toward Hiroma.

Hiroma looked back and forth between Kalira, Liotha, and the others. Hiroma's brow scrunched, the lines of thought racing behind her fluttering eyes. After a few more seconds, she looked back up at Kalira's outstretched arm.

"My mother is going to kill me..." she said, standing. "But by some grace of the makers, you've managed to convince Kalira. If you can do that, then I suppose I won't be left out. So, what's the plan?"

Liotha smiled at the two dragonesses, then turned to Mother and Taura, letting out a sigh of relief. Five of them against the might of Dro'Kal. She had no idea how much magic he'd absorbed, nor if the five of them would be enough, but it had to be. For the sake of her kind–for the sake of the very world itself, it had to be.

"Alright, so, here's the plan..."

CHAPTER SIX

BARGAIN

"Y ou knew Kalira and Hiroma were exactly who we needed, didn't you," Liotha said, giving Mother a sly look when the met the day after the meeting. The smile in reply told Liotha her assumption was correct. "Of course you knew. You know everything."

"As I told you, dearest, it's the job of a Scion to know the city's secrets, although in this case, I've known the talents of those two for some time now."

"But how did you know Kalira and Hiroma would come to the meeting?" Liotha asked, still a bit puzzled by that fact. So few had shown.

"One can never know for sure, but I had a hunch. Kalira and Hiroma have been two of our most loyal attendees. I presumed that would continue."

"I don't know why I question you," Liotha said, marveling at the elder dragoness's uncanny ability to always be right. "I'm not going to ask anymore. Just going to let you do what you do and trust it will all work out in the end."

"As well you should, Liotha, though I appreciate your trust in me." Mother offered a slight dip of her head, to which Liotha responded in like. "So, time for the next part of our plan. You're leaving soon?"

"Yes, just before dark. I'll head east and make it as far as I can before sunrise. I'll do a bit of scouting once I arrive, and then wait until sundown to enter the fortress. Hopefully, everything will be quiet and go smoothly. Once inside, I'll present our offer. I'll give them two days to give their response. I trust that's still good?" Liotha asked, assuming she already knew the answer.

"Yes, that should be enough time. We're still working on recruiting the others to our side. It's proven... difficult, but I am working on plans to provide a more poignant method of persuasion. I trust by the time you return with the good news, all will be set in motion."

Liotha nodded.

"Like I said, I won't question your methods," she said. "Just make sure they're ready when I get back. Hopefully, it will be with good news, and that we can move forward on schedule."

"I'm sure you will. Humans may be ravenous, vile creatures scrounging for whatever power they can take hold of, but they are veritably predictable. Offer them a chance at real power and I've no doubt they will be foaming at the mouth."

"That's the idea," Liotha scoffed. The thought of what she was about to do repulsed her, and she still wasn't sure if it would work, but they needed this piece for their plan to succeed. Worst case, if it did fail, it would only result in the humans' deaths and not their own kind.

"As far as our end of the bargain..." Liotha started, knowing Mother already knew what she was getting at.

"I'm working on that. By the time you get back, I'll have that ready as well."

"Very well," Liotha said. "I guess I should go get ready. I'll come find you as soon as I return."

"I look forward to it," Mother replied, bowing.

Liotha nodded with a smile.

She hastened her way to her room in Mother's abode. When she arrived, she began looking over the few things she had already packed. It was mostly just supplies for the flight, a tent, and a few other necessities. She didn't intend to linger and was traveling light.

She rummaged through her pack, grabbing a wrapped red cloth and unraveling it. Inside, the empty glass vial was still there. *Just making sure.* It was the most important item in her pack. It was how she was going to convince this human warlord that what she offered was the real deal. She still had no idea if it would work with humans. She hoped it wasn't just the shadow of hope she was chasing. She hoped the magic could be replicated.

Carefully, she wrapped it back up in the red cloth and placed it securely in the middle of the other things in her bag. Glancing over at her orb sitting on the small desk in her room, she sighed. *The pieces are falling into place.*

She closed her pack and slung it over her shoulder, taking one last look about the room before shutting the door behind her.

"May the winds carry you swiftly," came a voice from the shadows. Liotha didn't jump this time, merely turning to watch as Taura walked out to greet her.

"Thank you, Taura. Let's hope more than the winds are in my favor."

"Watch yourself, Liotha. Those humans cannot be trusted."

"I know. I will. They are simply a means to an end. Let's just hope they're as predictable as Mother believes, and that the magic can work on them."

"Mother knows best," Taura said with a grin. "But all the same, watch your back. I'd go with you, but–"

"Mother needs you here. I'll be fine," Liotha said, dipping her head to Taura. "Probably better we don't show up in a group, anyways."

As she rounded the corner on her way out, she glanced back, seeing nothing but shadows amongst the flickering torches. Liotha chuckled quietly to herself.

Time to disappear, myself.

***

It was nearly sunset when Liotha saw the green lands of men beyond the white peaks, the border of the seemingly endless mountains of Thousand Peaks finally giving way to the less frigid lands to the east. It was the first time she'd seen the Vale for herself.

Before recent events, Liotha had little care for the outside world. She'd been raised on stories of the wicked men who dwelt far to the east across the mountains. They'd been told to believe men were once their slaves, but due to the heinous acts of a traitor, they'd been set free, settling in the lands known as the Vale where they have thrived ever since. The stories said these men were vile creatures, devoid of magic, though they craved to somehow unlock its secrets for themselves. And if the stories were true, they'd even attempted to control it through science, though without the arcane in their blood, it was mostly futile.

Liotha knew the stories had been told in the dragons' favor, but most stories have a ring of truth to them. It was time for Liotha to find out for herself.

Glancing up at the sun, she noted there were only a few hours of daylight left. This would give her some time to land atop one of the last peaks, using her keen eyesight to glean what she could from a safe distance. The last thing she needed was the humans alerted to her presence.

Her energy was low, but not to the point of being dangerous. The flight had been longer than she'd expected, and a snowstorm delayed her around halfway. Playing it safe, she'd rested overnight and continued on this morning. This was good, as it meant she didn't need to rest just yet. She'd settle down, take a look, then perhaps take a nap and recover her strength for the night's activities.

She spotted the prime location—a peak on the edge of the mountains, one of the highest nearby and just the right distance to observe the lands below. There were other peaks a bit closer, but she deemed them too close and too low for comfort.

Settling down gently, she stayed in dragon form. She still had energy to expend, and her eyesight was even better in this form. Plus, this high up on the peaks, it was frigid, and her scales kept out the cold bite of the ever-constant wind.

As she peered down into the valley, she spotted a small village nestled amongst the rolling green hills stretching beyond the base of the mountains. The village was surrounded by green fields, many of which looked to contain various crops and other vegetation. Leafy trees formed a perimeter around the village and extended almost as far as her eyesight could see before opening up into more plains far beyond. Spotting nothing else notable, she turned her attention back to the town below.

A farming village. Mother's notes spoke of a local warlord. Surely, he's not there.

Her eyes narrowed as she scanned further, eventually drifting to the base of the mountains. After scanning a few times over, she was about to give up when she spotted it—a stone-grey structure that nearly blended into the hillside it was built against.

It was a castle, crude, yet the position was undoubtedly optimal. It appeared that perhaps a portion of the mountain had been carved out to provide additional shelter within its walls. And indeed, after watching for a bit longer, Liotha saw the forms of men moving about the fortress, some of them disappearing in and out of the dark spot in the mountain.

That must be it.

She continued to watch it for some time, noting several comings and goings down the hill and into the valley and town below. There was nothing significant, however, and Liotha soon found herself beginning to drift off.

Better make camp and settle down.

She scanned the hills for somewhere safe, a bit closer to the snowline. With what she'd brought, she'd be much too cold up here in her human skin. She noted the hills above the fortress were not occupied, and if she approached from the west, she should be able to land safely and approach the spot on foot. Stretching her wings, she lifted off and flew down the mountain, using the hills as cover until she came to a landing in the spot she'd estimated.

Shifting back into her human form, she continued from there on foot. It was cold, but bearable, only taking her a short while to make the trek down the hillside to where she'd set up her tent. She found a nice, flat spot to pitch it and got to work.

***

When Liotha opened her eyes, it was well past dark. It took several seconds for her eyes to adjust with how incredibly black the night was here. Even with her keen sight, she couldn't see much of anything.

Fortunately, once she climbed out of the small ravine she'd camped in and came to the top of a hill overlooking the valley, the moonlight grazing her pale skin, she could see enough to plot a path down the mountain. Wasting no time, she began her descent.

She passed the snowline in short time and descended into the pine trees as they began to grow in numbers. She lost sight of the fortress a handful of times but knew the direction. When she finally came out into a clearing, only a stone's throw from the fortress walls, she stopped and surveyed the area for any signs of activity. She spotted a few sleepy guards atop the crude walls, but otherwise it seemed quite calm.

Though the walls were crudely built, it seemed they had shored up their defenses well enough, making it difficult for intruders and unwelcome guests to wander inside. Difficult for non-magical beings, anyways.

Pulling her hood low over her head to hide her glowing eyes, she leapt up and grabbed onto a small stone outcropping some twenty feet above. It was small and slippery, but with her fingers morphing into claws, she was able to grab hold and launch herself upward to the top of the wall. She waited there, quietly listening to see if anyone had heard her. She was no master of stealth and would have easily been caught by a more attentive foe, but it seemed her presence so far remained undetected. That's when the smell of ale filled her nostrils.

Of course. What else to do up here on the edge of the world.

Ignoring the stench of ale, and now vomit, she propelled herself over the edge and scampered down the other side of the wall. Hiding behind a pile of crates, she peered out, looking for any sign of movement.

There was a large bonfire burning in the center of the open area, just beyond the dark entrance of the cave. Its light cast a glow on several men, most of whom appeared to be asleep. The two who were awake held cups in their hands, laughing amongst each other. One of them stood and pissed into the fire, sparking more laughs from the other.

Considering the two drunk men barely a threat, Liotha followed the wall to her right and crept silently toward the darkness of the cave, assuming that's where she'd find their leader. As she crept, one of the guards up on the wall started walking her way, passing overhead and continuing along. Liotha paused briefly, waited, and kept moving once he passed.

As she reached the edge of the darkness, Liotha stopped and used her sight to peer inside, her eyes shimmering a little brighter. Several torches lined the walls, and two illuminated a smaller entrance leading deeper inside. All was still, though she could hear voices coming from somewhere inside. Taking one last look around her, she crept forward, staying around the edges where the shadows lingered.

Stopping again inside the darkness near the smaller cave's entrance, she listened and waited. The voices were louder now, definitely coming from deeper within, though she still had a hard time distinguishing words.

She rushed through the light of the torches and disappeared deeper into the cave. As she moved, she noted several passages branching off on either side, the sounds of sleeping men coming from within.

Ignoring them, she pressed onward toward the voices coming from down the main tunnel. After a minute of walking, she came to where the tunnel opened into a much larger cavern. She immediately noticed several men talking to a larger man seated on a chair near the back wall, the ground sloping upward to give it a throne-like appearance. On the wall behind him hung dozens of dragon skulls of various shapes and sizes. Lesser dragons, she assumed, as her kind rarely strayed this far east. But even so, the sight still made her stomach twist into an uncomfortable knot.

"The villages are growing less and less willing to pay tribute, Garn," said the larger of the two men to the man on the chair, Liotha noting a large spear leaning against the side of it. "The last dragon sighting was several moons ago. Hard to collect a protection tax when they don't think they need protecting."

The man they referred to as Garn brushed his hand across his face, a look of anxiety clear in his features.

"What about the smaller towns up north? And Northreach beyond that? What did you find out?" asked Garn.

"We've visited all the villages up north–it's all the same. No dragons, no tax. We tried telling them they could appear at any time, but it didn't make much difference. And based on what we saw, Northreach is going to be a problem," said the smaller man.

"Why?" asked Garn, lifting his head and squinting at the man.

"The Capital sent troops to guard the port. At least four dozen, by our count. They will certainly not pay with Solantrian knights present."

"Bah!' grunted Garn, rubbing his face with both hands. "Always wanting to be left alone until the dragons come knocking. Remind me why we decided to settle down out here on the damned edge of the world..."

"Far from the Capital, Chief. At least here we don't have to worry about them showing up at our gate."

Garn looked up at the man with an annoyed expression.

"I know why, you oaf. But what's the point avoiding the Capital's gaze if we starve? Our luck has gotten worse every season. If things don't change, we may have to give up this venture and go back to our old lives. Do you want to be a farmer again, Vornir?"

"No, Chief. I do not."

"Well, then you better figure out how we're going to survive out here. Can't collect a protection tax if we don't have any dragons to kill. Might have to resort to... less savory means of persuasion."

"I– I'm sure it won't come to that, Chief. We'll figure something out," the smaller man chimed in. Vornir looked at him, then back to Garn, nodding his agreement.

"I'm exhausted," Garn sighed, slouching forward. "We'll reconvene in the morning and discuss our plans."

Liotha watched from her hiding place as Vornir and the smaller man exited through the same entrance she'd entered. Once out of sight, she turned her attention back to Garn, who continued to sit in his chair, his head bowed low. *Is he just going to sleep there?*

As the echo of the others' voices faded away, Liotha moved around the edge of the cavern, keeping out of sight, though there was little stirring from Garn. After a minute, she stopped, standing quietly in the shadows off to Garn's right, watching him. His breathing was heavy, but she didn't think he was sleeping.

Just as Liotha was about to step out of the shadows, Garn sat up and pounded his fist on the arm of his chair.

"Blast this damned fate," he said out loud. Liotha could hear the angst in his tone.

So much for warlord, she thought to herself. *These are the so-called drag-on-killers? More like a ragged band of thieves and pillagers. Maybe I'm wasting my time here...*

"There's got to be more than this worthless existence," Garn continued. "To scrounge for scraps like dogs. The gods themselves abandoned us long ago. I don't blame them."

Liotha thought for a moment. This was perfect. He was desperate. She could use that, even if these men didn't seem to be quite what she'd been told. But Mother's notes said these were the men. Perhaps, there was more to them than meets the eye. She glanced up at the dragon heads above him. They obviously had some skill. If her plan worked, she could make these men something so much more.

She pulled a dagger out of her belt and pricked the end of her finger, removing the glass vial from around her neck and filling it until it was mostly full. She wrapped a small piece of cloth she'd prepared around her finger, tying it off at the end. She tucked the necklace back inside her shirt and stood.

"Who needs the gods anyways," Liotha said from the shadows.

Garn stood abruptly, grabbing his spear and spinning in her direction.

"Who's there? Show yourself!"

"Easy now, Garn Dragon-Killer. I've not come to harm you."

"Is that so?" he said, keeping his spear pointed into the darkness. "Come into the light and I shall decide that for myself."

"No need to get violent. I'll come into the light. Just promise me you'll listen to what I have to say," Liotha said. She moved forward slowly, raising her hands up, her hood still covering her face.

"Who are you? How did you sneak in here?"

"I've come to offer you a deal."

"You didn't answer my question."

"Most of your men are asleep, and the ones awake reek of ale. It wasn't that hard."

Garn glanced sideways toward the exit, a slight hesitation as he contemplated her words, his face betraying his irritation.

"We don't get many visitors out this way, which makes your presence all that much more concerning. Remove your hood," Garn demanded, quickly regaining his composure.

"Very well," Liotha said, seeing she wasn't going to get much further without conceding.

As she lifted her hood, she kept her head bowed forward. Slowly, she looked up at Garn. As soon as her eyes met his, she saw his expression change. It wasn't an expression of fear or anger, but something else, like he was assessing her in a new light. It unsettled her how calm he remained.

"An elder dragon, eh? Haven't seen one of your kind in a long time. Haven't *killed* one of your kind in a long time. That explains how you got past my men so easily, but still doesn't quite explain *who* you are, nor why you are here."

"Who I am is of little importance," Liotha said. "Back home, I'm nobody. It's what I'm trying to do that's important, and that is why I'm here."

"What do the affairs of elder dragons have to do with us?"

"Tell me, Dragon-Killer. Do you know of our Wyrmlord, Dro'Kal?"

"We've heard rumors. Some say he's been seen outside your lands of late. Some say he's even laid siege to cities in the north across the sea. But these are just rumors, and they mean little to us here on the edge of the Vale. What of it?"

"They are more than just rumors. Dro'Kal is consuming the world's magic. If left unchecked, he could consume the beating heart of Velasia itself."

"So what? Why should we care. Magic is of no use to us. You should know that. Plus, there is little magic in these lands." Garn relaxed a little, loosening his grip on his spear and waving one hand toward the exit of the cavern.

"The magical leylines stretch across this world, even in the Vale. Eventually, he will come for them. Even if he doesn't, once too much magic is gone, the world will begin to decay. If that happens, it will be too late. All realms will be swallowed up."

Liotha saw the hints of concern stretch across Garn's hardened face–the first since their conversation started. Her words seemed to have struck a chord.

"What do you want with us, then? What is this deal?" Garn questioned.

"You said you were tired of this life. Tired of scrounging for scraps. I heard you speak of your troubles with the others." Liotha saw Garn's eyes dart sideways again. "What if I told you, I could offer you a seat at a table the humans have been trying to sit at since the beginning of time?"

"I'm listening," he said, narrowing his eyes, as if he were trying to decipher the intent behind her words.

"What if I told you," Liotha said, "magic is not as far out of reach as you might believe?"

"Magic? Speak plainly, dragon. How can you offer magic? And you must expect something in return."

"I do," Liotha said. "There is no guarantee of success, and to succeed, we will require your aid in ending Dro'Kal."

"This Dro'Kal," Garn said. "If he's consumed magic like you say, he must be immensely powerful. How do we know this isn't a futile effort?"

"He is, indeed, powerful, but we have a plan. The pieces are falling into place. You are one of the last pieces."

"And what assurance do we have you are not just using us to further your own ends?" Garn asked.

Liotha hesitated for a moment. She hadn't been prepared to answer that question. *The man is smart–much smarter than I'd originally taken him for.*

"I told you. The fate of the world may be at stake. Despite living far across the mountains, we still share the same world. We're going to try to stop him with or without your aid. If you don't want the power I offer, I can simply disappear and leave you to continue this miserable existence for as long as you think you can. Or, you can accept what I offer, gaining a power all the lands of men will covet."

Liotha paused, looking up at the skulls of her kin on the wall. This gave her an idea. "Most of these skulls are of lesser dragons, no?"

Garn glanced upward with a curious expression, then back to her and nodded. "Aye. Most of them."

"With the power I offer, you'd have a chance to kill one of the strongest dragons to have ever lived. Just imagine what a trophy like that would look like hanging on your wall."

Liotha saw the spark of desire in Garn's eyes at the mention of that. *Gotcha.*

Garn placed the butt of his spear on the ground, his eyes darting back and forth. He looked at Liotha for a long, awkward moment without saying anything.

"Tell me everything, dragon," he finally said. "Every detail of your plan, how this power works, and what you will require of my men. If I sense even the slightest hint of deceit, I will end you here and now."

Liotha paused momentarily, a slight hint of fear creeping into her bones. She had underestimated the man, and she believed she was in very real danger if she couldn't convince him to trust her. Fortunately, she'd come prepared.

"Even better, how about I show you," Liotha said, emanating as much confidence as she could muster as she pulled the necklace out from around her neck. She held it up in the dim light of the cavern in front of her, the small glass vial dangling at its end. She stared past it at Garn, his eyes focused on it from across the empty space, hypnotized by the dull, red glow within. "Would you like to be the first to taste this power it is that I offer?"

CHAPTER SEVEN

POWER

In the days after Liotha's return from the human lands, they'd laid the final pieces of their trap. Their rumors of a new font of power detected on the fringes of human lands spread quickly, and it wasn't long before Mother Ere'daina confirmed it had spread through the upper echelons of court, finally reaching Dro'Kal's goons. And if the news had reached them, it was certain Dro'Kal knew. It was only a matter of time before they headed out, the fake leyline their destination.

When Mother heard whispers of another excursion being planned, she sent Liotha and the others ahead. They set up camp upon their arrival, and as soon as it was done, Liotha laid down in her tent to send her message to Garn.

It was called *aninexum*–thought connection. Because of Garn's successful transformation, Liotha could now establish a mind connection with him over shorter distances. She'd told him she would do so ahead of time, hoping the intrusion wouldn't be too alarming.

Their camp should've been within range, and after a short while, though faint, she felt his presence. Reaching for it, she eventually found her way inside his mind.

It is nearly time.

We are ready, Garn replied.

Good. How fast can you get here?

Before dark.

They will likely need to rest once they arrive. A good time to strike, if you can make it before they recover.

We'll be there.

How many will you be bringing?

Enough...

Liotha felt her connection fading. She was too tired and did not want to push herself too far. Performing the magic had already been risky.

Very well. Tonight, she finished, severing the connection.

Now, all there was to do was wait and rest. She fell asleep within minutes.

***

Liotha felt a gentle nudge on her arm, opening her eyes to see Taura leaning over her.

"They are coming," she said.

Liotha nodded, sitting up as Taura exited the tent. She rubbed the sleep out of her eyes and rose to her feet. She wasn't fully recharged, but she felt much better. It would be enough.

Exiting the tent, she saw the others rousing from their own rest. Spotting Taura by the edge of the cliff, she came up to stand beside her, noting the sun was already on its descent toward the western horizon.

"How many?" Liotha asked, straining her eyes. She saw the dots, but not well enough to discern an accurate count.

"I count seven," Taura said. "A few less than we expected. That bodes well. Our... *friends* are on the way?"

"Yes."

"How many?" Taura asked.

"He didn't say. Let's hope it's enough."

"Let's hope."

Kalira and Hiroma came up and joined them on the edge of the cliff.

"The moment of truth," Kalira said. "Are the *others* here yet?"

"Not yet," Liotha said, fidgeting. She looked up at the sky with concern. There were still a few hours of daylight left.

"They are necessary for this to work," Kalira added.

"They'll be here," Liotha said, her tone abrupt. She was grateful to have Kalira's help, but the dragoness had been a thorn in her side nearly every step of the way, constantly questioning Liotha and all aspects of her plan. Liotha let it slide for the most part, but it was beginning to wear on her. And now, with the weight of everything coming down to bear, Kalira was *still* questioning.

"I hope so," Kalira said, her own tone a bit on edge. She eyed Hiroma, cocked her head to the side, and the two of them walked off to attend to their own preparations.

"Don't let her get to you, Liotha," Taura said once they were out of earshot. "That's just how Kalira is. She's even questioned Mother on many occasions. You get used to it."

"The price of leadership, I suppose," Liotha acknowledged, to which Taura nodded in agreement. Liotha felt a slight tinge of energy in the back of her skull. Turning around, she looked toward the peaks to the east.

"Our friends are getting closer," she said. Taura nodded again, turning to look east with Liotha.

"I suppose we best prepare ourselves, then," she said, placing her hand on Liotha's shoulder, giving Liotha a firm nod before taking her leave down a path taking her down below the cliff.

Liotha watched her with a smile. It was the first time Liotha had ever felt the stern dragoness be so genuine with her. It was nice. She was grateful that Mother had insisted on Taura coming as her escort, and her protector, should anything go wrong. Liotha hoped it wouldn't come to that, but felt a little safer, nonetheless.

Liotha turned her gaze up, taking one last look at the forms of Dro'Kal and his consort approaching, the setting sun behind them as their dots became distinguishable outlines. With a heavy sigh, she turned and followed Taura down the path. It was going to be a long evening.

Liotha and the others watched as the forms of Dro'Kal and his companions descended toward the earth, each taking their human skin as their feet touched the ground. Through the trees, Liotha only caught scattered glimpses of the others who'd accompanied him. The ones she could see appeared weary. Dro'Kal, however, seemed fine, moving as though he'd just woken from a nap. His limit was far beyond what any normal dragon should be able to bear. Perhaps he had figured out a way to circumvent the gods' curse after all.

As Dro'Kal wandered about the area, they watched as the others began setting up camp. Liotha could hear their talking, but it was mostly an incoherent murmur. Even if Dro'Kal didn't need rest, they did. Apparently, he did not allow them to share in his gluttony. Liotha was not surprised by that, but it did make what they were about to do seem a little harder. She wondered if any of them even had much choice in the matter, though she knew there were plenty others who served willingly.

Turning her attention back to the Wyrmlord, she watched him as he continued to scan the surrounding area. Though she'd seen it before, writhing underneath his skin, this was the first time she'd seen an obvious display of his power. It was simple, to not need rest after such a long flight, but she had a feeling before the day was over, they were going to see a whole lot more.

Liotha continued to watch as Dro'Kal wandered further away from the group. She glanced beside her, exchanging questioning looks with the others.

"He's... leaving them," Hiroma said. "Should we–?"

"No, not yet. Garn is close, but he's not close enough. Just wait."

They watched for several more minutes, Dro'Kal eventually disappearing beyond the trees in the valley below. They waited for a few more minutes, but there was no sign of his return.

"He must be looking for the font on his own," Liotha said. Feeling a sense of urgency, she closed her eyes and reached out with her mind, searching for Garn's presence. He was getting closer, but still on the move. Just as she was about to reach out to him, she felt the touch of a hand on her arm.

She opened her eyes to see Taura gently shaking her head. She was pointing down into the valley. Liotha's eyes followed.

Dro'Kal had come back, and he was storming up toward one of the tents. He stopped, waiting outside. When no one stirred, he yelled. From where Liotha and the others watched, they could hear him clearly.

"I sense no magic here," he shouted. "Why have you wasted my time, Li'rael?"

"Are you sure, my Lord? It was supposed to be here. I was promised by–"

"You should have confirmed, whelp. I do not like wasting my time. We should leave."

By now, the others were stirring from their tents, though no one dared approach the confrontation.

"We– we need our rest, Lord," Li'rael said, almost begging.

"Ach!" Dro'Kal scoffed. "Weaklings, all of you. Fine, rest then, but we leave at sundown." Dro'Kal stormed off before the other drake could respond, walking a dozen paces and then shifting, his massive form taking flight and quickly disappearing past the mountain beyond.

"He's leaving," Kalira said. "What do we do?"

"He'll be back at sundown," Liotha replied. "That should give us the time we need to prepare."

"Liotha's right," Taura said. "We should kill the others while he's away."

A bit taken aback, Liotha met Taura's gaze. She knew they were a threat and needed to be taken care of. It would make dealing with Dro'Kal much easier, but to kill them in their sleep? That felt wrong.

"I don't know–"

"This plan is already fragile, Liotha. With them out of the way, that's one less factor to worry about. You know I'm right," Taura said.

"Very well," Liotha sighed. "I suppose you're right, but let me go meet Garn and escort him to the camp–just to ensure things don't go badly for us."

"Find him quickly," Taura acknowledged. "We will move closer and wait for your signal. Best to give them a few to fall asleep, anyways."

Liotha nodded, stepping away from the group and heading toward a nearby clearing. Once there, she let loose her energy, transforming into her true self. With a rush of her wings, she lifted off, taking care to stay low, just in case Dro'Kal was still within sight of the area.

Spotting no sign of the wyrm, she hastened onward in the direction of the human lands. After a few minutes, she began to feel the pull of Garn's presence below. Not wanting to approach in her true form, she doubled back and landed ahead of them where she waited for them to approach.

After a short while, she heard the sound of feet and the crunch of snow. Emerging from her hiding spot, she stepped into the path before them, all of them raising their spears at her–all except Garn.

"So few?" Liotha said, loud enough for all to hear. By her count, there were only twenty.

Garn looked back over his men, then turned to her with a solemn face.

"As you said, some would not survive. These are the strongest–or luckiest," he said with a smirk. "No matter. We will slay your wyrm. Where is he?"

"Their camp is just in the valley beyond," she said, pointing up the slopes behind her. "He left, storming off in anger. He knows there's no leyline here. But the others, they need their rest. We have a short while before he returns. A short while to... eliminate those he brought with him."

"You hear that, boys," Garn yelled with another smirk. "It's time to put this new strength to good use. Let's go kill us some dragons."

Cheers rang out from the column behind Garn as they began to move, following their leader. Liotha's stomach turned at the thought of what she was about to let him do.

"No offense," Garn said as he walked past Liotha, the corner of his mouth raised ever so slightly, the men following him casting wary glances at Liotha as they passed.

She could smell the taint on them. It filled her nostrils, making her feel sick.

"A means to an end," she said under her breath once the column had passed.

It was clear Garn's men were strong by their quick pace up the smaller mountain and down the other side. It wasn't long before Liotha spotted the tents along the valley floor. She caught up with Garn and slowed their march as they neared the edge of the trees. Using her sight, she scanned the opposite side for Taura and the others. After a few moments, she spotted them amongst the shadows of the trees.

Locking eyes with Taura, she nodded. *Ready?*

Ready, Taura replied.

"Let's go, quietly," Liotha said, turning to Garn. "No need to wake them if we can get this over with quickly."

Garn smiled and nodded, turning to those directly behind him and waving his hand forward, bringing his finger up to his lips.

His men moved slowly out into the open area, spears raised and moving in near silence. For men, Liotha was impressed. Despite their ragged appearance, it was clear Mother's notes had been accurate about them. They moved and carried themselves like real warriors. Perhaps they did stand a chance against Dro'Kal after all.

As they surrounded the tents, several at each, Liotha followed, arriving in the middle. She met Garn's eyes and hesitated for a moment. She knew what he was after, but she couldn't give it. She didn't know these drakes—didn't know if they had families, or children. Her eyes dropped and her hands instinctively moved to her stomach. The bump was getting bigger.

Glancing back up, she saw they were proceeding without her approval. She closed her eyes, heard the spears strike flesh, heard the grunts and gurgle of blood being spilt, smelled the blood of her kin. Though it was not her holding the weapon, she knew their blood was on her hands.

There was a jump in her belly, followed by a small pulse of energy. Another cry rang out from a nearby tent. It was a voice she recognized.

"Stop!" Liotha called out, spinning toward the sound.

What she saw in that moment caused both fear and anger at the same time. It was Hel'aren, a spear lodged in his side, horror-filled eyes staring up at the man holding the spear. And then he saw her.

Something changed inside Liotha as their eyes locked. She had not expected to ever see her mate again. She'd spent many nights full of dark dreams, of the terrible things she wanted to do to him. But now, with his blood seeping onto the ground, the pain and pleading look in his eyes, the cry for help, she did not know what to do. She wanted him dead, but at the same time, he was the father of her children.

Garn, seeming to notice the dilemma, came up beside Liotha.

"Do you know this one?" he asked.

Yes, she said in her mind. But the word would not come out. She just stared at Hel'aren. He stretched his hand up to her, begging, the last remnant of a life that now seemed ages ago. *He chose his side.*

"No... I do not," she said, looking away from her mate and up at Garn, her heart hardening with every word. She blushed, her cheeks growing warm. Whether it was in anger or shame, she did not know. She didn't care.

"Lioth–" Hel'aren cried out, cut short by the wave of Garn's hand, the sound of flesh ripping, blood spilling forth as the spear was removed, then struck into Hel'aren again, silencing his cries forever.

Liotha never looked back. She turned and saw Taura standing toward the back of the group, a solemn expression directed her way. There was an apparent understanding there as their eyes met. Liotha wanted nothing more than to run and hug her. She needed to feel the warmth of another's embrace. Her heart and mind felt cold now, her legs weak. She took a careful step forward.

An ear-piercing screech echoed through the valley. Liotha's eyes widened, her body trembling from the reverberations of the sound. She looked up, seeing the form of Dro'Kal barreling down toward them from above the mountain.

"Positions!" Garn howled. "Spread out. Clear the landing."

Garn's men scattered, moving out of the open area and taking positions along the edge of the trees. As they did, Liotha heard Taura shouting her name, felt her firm grip take hold of her, tugging her out of the open area. Before she fully realized what had happened, she was hiding under cover with Taura and the others.

Another roar, Dro'Kal's shadow filling the open space as he drew closer. Liotha felt the presence of his power now. It was terrifying.

"It's massive..." she murmured, not fully realizing she'd said the words out loud.

"What?" asked Taura.

"His power... it's– it's far beyond what I thought." Liotha stuttered, her mind still numb from the waves of energy flowing over her. She'd felt his power before, sensed it lying dormant under the surface, but now it was loose for all to bear witness.

"Yes," said Taura. "It is... impressive, but Liotha, you must focus. We have a task at hand–to ensure it ends here and now."

Liotha looked into Taura's eyes as she spoke. How could she be so calm in the face of such power? Liotha envied her confidence and steel nerves. Taura continued to speak, the words muffled by the voices in Liotha's head, the waves of Dro'Kal's power, and the wind now howling through the trees. Liotha saw the face of her mate. *Monsters*, she heard in her head, Mother Ere'daina's voice.

There was a slam, a furious gust of wind ripping through the trees, debris and dirt hitting them, wrenching Liotha from her thoughts. She looked up to see Dro'Kal now on the ground, still in dragon form, his head sweeping from side to side.

"Where are you, little birds," he roared. "I knew it was a trap as soon as I smelled the stink of the humans. Seems you took the bait of my sleeping lackeys. No matter, their deaths were meaningless."

Meaningless? Liotha felt even more ashamed by his words.

"But tell me, Liotha..."

Liotha gasped. *How did he know?*

"How did you convince these wretches to help you? What did you promise them? Fame? Glory?" he said, pausing and sniffing. "Power? Heh, heh, heh," he laughed, deep and throaty. "But you didn't really tell them what they were truly up against, did you?"

Liotha glanced at Taura and the others. She squinted, trying to spot Garn and his men in the shadows of the woods on the opposite side of Dro'Kal.

"Or perhaps... even you didn't know. Perhaps whomever you're working with didn't tell you, either? Heh, heh, heh," he laughed again. "Nevertheless, we are here, now. All will be revealed. So, who wants to die first?"

Liotha spotted Garn stepping out of the woods, a hundred or so feet to Dro'Kal's left.

"I'm here, dragon" he called out, Dro'Kal's neck snapping in his direction. "Although I think you'll find it's you who's underestimated us," Garn said with a confident smile.

What is he doing? Liotha thought. *Going to get himself killed.*

Dro'Kal laughed again, this time even louder and deeper.

"Ah, the arrogance. How predictable. A bold claim for one with so small a stature, and no power to overcome his insignificance. But very well, you may die first." Dro'Kal took a step forward.

"Ah, but you see, dragon, that's where you're wrong," Garn said, his smile growing bigger.

Almost faster than Liotha could see, Garn pulled his spear back and released it into the air. In a split second, it zipped past Dro'Kal's face, grazing his cheek, ripping a chunk of skin out. The dragon seemed to be caught off guard by the sheer speed the human had moved.

Dro'Kal reeled from the attack, spinning away and then circling back to face Garn, though there was a bit more distance between them now.

"WHAT IS THIS?" he roared. "What have you done, Liotha?"

He moved his head from side to side, eyeing the woods. When his gaze passed where Liotha and the others were hiding, she cringed and shielded her eyes. She heard him grunt in frustration and opened them again.

"Keep hiding, coward. I'll deal with you after these... abominations!"

Dro'Kal lunged forward, his massive legs sending shockwaves through the ground with each step, his limbs pulsing with a surge of energy. Liotha felt her heart skip a beat, still trying to come to terms with his sheer power.

She watched as he charged straight for Garn, the man continuing to stand his ground confidently. *How can he be so calm in the face of such terror? If he can do it...*

Dro'Kal drew closer and closer, coming nearly within range to snap at Garn with his powerful jaws, when again Garn moved with an inhuman speed. He dove underneath Dro'Kal's hulking form, dodging between his legs and avoiding his claws, coming to a roll back up on his feet behind the dragon and sprinting after his spear in the distance. As Garn moved, Dro'Kal continued barreling toward the trees, unable to stop himself. As he slammed into them, Liotha saw several men jump on top of him, stabbing with spears, small tears opening, red spewing forth.

Dro'Kal roared, though whether it was in pain or increased anger, Liotha couldn't tell. He shook violently, the men unable to hold on, most landing on their feet. The blood, it seemed, had produced a more potent effect than Liotha had expected.

Hiroma and Kalira stood, moving to join in the fight. Taura stepped up and blocked their path.

"What are you doing? Aren't we going to help?" Kalira asked in confusion.

"No, we're not," Liotha said, looking up at Taura. Kalira turned to her, looking even more confused.

"I thought–"

"The real plan was never for us to fight with them. They are the distraction, only meant to push Dro'Kal to his limit... if such a thing exists," Liotha said, standing to join them.

"You said we were here to stop Dro'kal–to end his rule. If they die, then what?" Kalira asked.

"We never told you the real plan because we needed to be sure he would not hear of it," Liotha said. "Theoretically, if Dro'Kal uses up enough of his power, he will need to rest. You saw him when they arrived. He needed no rest. We needed something to ensure he would be pushed to his limits. That's what they are here to do, nothing more. It's unlikely any of them will survive, but hopefully they will live long enough to exhaust his power. Then, once he's resting, we enact our real plan."

"Which is?" Hiroma asked.

"To trap his mind in the Dream."

Both dragoness's eyes grew wide.

"The Dream? And how exactly do we do that?" Kalira asked.

"*Somb'ulatura*. Dreamwalking. I've been practicing. When he goes to sleep, I'll try to enter his dreams. With any luck, he'll follow me. I'll lead him beyond his own consciousness, and once he's far enough, you will help pull me out. If it works, he'll end up trapped in there forever. Then, we figure out where to hide him and you–" Liotha said, pointing to Hiroma, "will help me figure out how to siphon his magic back into the world."

Kalira and Hiroma looked at each other, doubt written all over their faces.

"And will this actually work?" Kalira asked, turning back to Liotha.

"In theory..." Liotha said timidly, trying not to blush.

"In theory?" Kalira exclaimed. "This is madness."

The sound of the fighting intensified, all of them turning to see Dro'Kal taking to the sky, two bodies of slain men lying in the wake of the dust cloud he left behind. Liotha saw Garn and several others helping other injured men back into the trees, all the while watching the sky for what Dro'Kal would do next.

The wyrm circled momentarily, then directed his descent back down toward the forest where the men were hiding. His maw opened wide, a dull red glow growing steadily as he dove, slowly shifting into a brilliant yellow. The men in his wake didn't stand a chance.

A few seconds later, it was as if hell opened up and swallowed the forest whole.

Liotha watched in stunned silence as the forest opposite them was incinerated in a manner of seconds. She heard cries of agony, saw a few men stumble out of the woods, making it only a few feet before their flesh melted and burning piles of bones fell to the earth.

Liotha had known Garn's purpose the whole time. It had been her idea, in part. But seeing them dying now, the doing of her own schemes. It horrified her. Had her heart hardened so much from who she was just a short time ago?

She reached up to her face, feeling the rough edges of healed skin where the scorch marks had once been, now hidden under her mask. She had survived her fire. Those men... they would not.

Dro'Kal continued to spew flames, his neck turning toward their side of the ravine, beginning to set the forest ablaze all around. Ashamed as she was, Liotha and the others needed to retreat, lest they meet the same fate.

"Let's go," shouted Taura, the roar of flames growing ever closer.

Fortunately, there was a path up the side of the rocky crag behind them. Whether it was by fate, or by Taura's own design, Liotha did not know, but she praised their good fortune.

Within minutes, they'd ascended the rocky path and were safely back up on the cliffside above the gruesome battle scene. Dro'Kal had finished his rage now and was scouring the flames, looking for any signs of life.

"They're all dead, aren't they?" Hiroma asked through bated breaths.

"They must be," Kalira huffed. "Did you see that? I've never seen anyone spew forth that much fire, and yet he still maintains his true form. How is this possible?"

Liotha shook her head, unable to answer as she stared down into the valley. Did his power have no limit? Had he already achieved the impossible?

"Look!" Taura said, pointing to Dro'Kal.

Liotha's eyes focused. She saw Dro'Kal staggering, shaking his head back and forth like something was wrong. He clawed the dirt with his foot, then lifted his head and let loose another roar. As he turned around, his head up, his eyes landed on the cliffside where they were standing.

When their eyes locked, Liotha felt her heart stop. A shiver ran down her spine.

Dro'Kal roared again, raised his wings, and launched himself into the air. The rage within his eyes bore into Liotha's soul as he headed straight for them.

CHAPTER EIGHT

CHASE

L iotha's heart pounded in her chest as she and the others dove below a mountain peak and took a sharp left down into the valley, trying desperately to shake Dro'Kal as he gradually gained on them.

She looked back over her shoulder, a momentary glimpse, spotting the other dragonesses close on her tail, Taura just behind and to her left. They glided as close to the treetops as they dared, trying to stay as low as possible, hoping that perhaps Dro'Kal would zoom past and not notice they'd veered off. Daylight was drawing to a close, and down in the small valley next to the mountains, it was darker.

There was a bend in the valley up ahead as it wrapped around another large mountain and between the next through a narrow cliffside. Liotha looked over at Taura, the look in her eyes indicative she had the same idea. Not wanting to reach out with her mind, just in case Dro'Kal was able to sense it, she nodded to Taura.

As the gap approached, Liotha rose slightly, tipping her left wing down toward the tops of the trees. A taller tree clipped her wing and she winced, but held steady, zooming around the side of the mountain in a breakneck speed, trying to leave enough room for Taura and the others on her inside while making sure her exterior wing didn't graze the rocky cliff.

As they rounded the corner and came into view of the wide-open space beyond, Liotha scanned the space before them. There was no sign of Dro'Kal. Glancing backward, she looked at Taura, then back to the other two, nodding to them.

Liotha saw the flash of light a split second before she felt the surge of energy above. She dived to the side, barely in time to dodge Dro'Kal's flames as he bore down on them from above the mountain they'd just circled. The giant ball of flame smashed into the cliffside above, sending showers of stones downward, some of which could do some serious damage should they hit her. She lost sight of her friends as the massive wave of fire and stone fell behind her, several rocks narrowly missing her while other, smaller stones pelted her backside. Fire continued to spew from above, Dro'Kal drawing closer and closer as he bore down after her. She could now feel the intensity of the heat along her spine.

Though fire was less of a threat in her dragon form, she'd seen what he'd done to the forest. She didn't want to chance it. Trying desperately to avoid the encroaching flames, she swayed back and forth, all the while trying to steal quick glances behind her to see where the others had gone.

A screech from above and the flames stopped. Liotha craned her neck to look up, spotting a shadow clinging to Dro'Kal's side.

Taura.

Liotha spun, circling back to try and help her friend. She saw them struggling as she approached, Dro'Kal spinning through the air to try and shake her as Taura sank her teeth into his neck, her claws holding on as best she could. She seemed but a child against his massive form.

Dro'Kal let out a deafening roar. A pulse of energy flashed all around them, sending Taura flying off. A second later, as Liotha continued to climb, she felt the shockwave.

It stunned her for a second, and she lost her upward momentum. Her mind grasped at straws, trying to understand what had just happened. Somehow, he'd just sent out a blast of energy from his core.

Liotha regained herself and turned back up to see Taura falling steadily, seeming as if she'd been knocked completely unconscious. Dro'Kal was falling after her, just seconds behind. He, too, looked like he might be unconscious.

Liotha pushed herself to try and get to her friend's aid but wasn't sure she was going to make it.

Taura was seconds from the ground when she regained consciousness and snapped her wings open, just in time to slow her descent. But it was too late, Dro'Kal's limp form catching up and pushing her down toward the ground. Liotha watched as they disappeared from view into the forest below, Taura trying desperately to get out of the way before she was crushed by the impact. Liotha heard the crash and saw the wave of wind whipping through the trees in the vicinity.

Liotha gasped, pushing herself even harder, praying Taura had been able to break free before the impact.

She slowed on approach, looking for a safe spot to land amongst the clearing the two dragons had just made. Avoiding the snapped remains of tree trunks, she landed and rolled, shifting back to her human form and instantly beginning to search for Taura amidst the cloud of snow that had been flung into the air.

She spotted Dro'Kal's still limp form through the settling snow and darted toward it, her eyes scanning for any sign of Taura. As she rounded the huge drake, his body began to slowly shift back to his human form. As it did, Liotha spotted Taura's body close by. She, too, lay deathly still.

Rushing over, she knelt down, shoving Dro'Kal aside, now fully transformed back into his human skin.

"Taura, Taura," she called out.

She heard beating wings behind her and turned, seeing Kalira and Hiroma approaching.

"Help, Taura's hurt," she shouted to them as they morphed and sprinted over.

"She was pinned underneath him. I'm not sure..."

"Move aside," Hiroma said, kneeling down beside them in the snow. She laid her head on Taura's chest, listening for several seconds. "It's still beating, but it's slowed. The fall must have knocked her unconscious."

"What about him?" Kalira asked, examining Dro'Kal's lifeless body.

"I think he's alive, but whatever that was that he did... I– I think he used the last of his energy up."

"Well, he didn't turn feral. That's a good sign, at least, but I don't want to find out the hard way that he's going to wake up. We should perform the rite now while we have the chance."

"What about Taura, she's–"

"She's right," Taura moaned, slowly opening her eyes.

Liotha knelt back down beside Taura and put her hand on her shoulder.

"Are you okay?" Liotha asked. "I thought for sure you were–"

"Dead?" Taura asked, a slight smirk forming. "I'm not that easy to kill. But everything hurts and I–" Taura winced, unable to finish the words as she tried to sit up. She was clutching her side. "Rib's busted, maybe more. Yeah, definitely more."

"Alright, so... we just going to stand here or do this thing?" Kalira asked, drawing looks from both Taura and Liotha.

"She's–" Liotha started.

"–not vital to this part, Liotha," Taura said, cutting her off. "I did my part. It's your and Kalira's turn now. And like she said, we don't know how much time we have. So, get to it. I'll be fine."

Liotha showed her skepticism as she looked at Taura, but eventually nodded after getting a prodding look back from the tough dragoness.

"Alright, let's get to it. I guess here is as good as anywhere. Hiroma, can you start making a fire while Kalira and I prepare? It's going to get cold out here with night setting in, and I personally don't want to escape the Dream only to wake up frozen to death."

Hiroma nodded after getting a nod from Taura and stood, quickly setting about gathering all the scattered wood from the crash. While she worked, Liotha and Kalira began clearing a spot for both her and Dro'Kal's body. She didn't want to lie in the snow, and she needed to lie next to him to ensure she could find his dreams more easily. It wasn't a lot of prep work, but Liotha also needed to calm her mind and focus, especially after what had just transpired.

Once her spot was clear, Liotha sat down and made herself comfortable while Kalira prepared Dro'Kal in his spot next to her. She eyed Taura one last time, getting another nod through a wince of pain.

Within a few minutes, Liotha's mind was beginning to calm, just as she started to hear the crackle of the nearby fire. Opening her eyes, she looked over and saw Kalira was finishing up, Dro'Kal lying still just a few feet away.

It felt odd to Liotha, having him so close. He looked calm and peaceful in his current state. Because he'd used so much of his power, he almost looked normal. She wondered what he might have been like before all this had happened. Perhaps, in another life, things could have been different.

Shaking her head, she pushed aside the invasive thoughts. No matter how it had started, it was his choice. He'd chosen his path long ago, and nothing could change it now. He was perhaps the greatest monster of them all. Hopefully, after tonight, no more.

"Ready?" Kalira asked, breaking Liotha's gaze away from the wyrm.

"Yes," Liotha said. "Let's do this."

Liotha laid down, making herself as comfortable as she could on the cold ground. It wasn't ideal, but she was already starting to feel the warmth of the fire. It would have to do.

She turned her head to the side, seeing Taura staring intently at her through gritted teeth as she warmed herself by the fire. One last nod and Liotha turned her head, looking up at the stars above. After staring at them for a few more seconds, she closed her eyes, saying goodbye to the real world as she began her descent into the Dream.

Within the darkness of the Dream world, Liotha wandered, searching for Dro'Kal's presence. At first, all she felt was cold. She pushed her discomfort away and focused. After a few more moments of searching, she felt it amongst the darkness.

The closer she got to it, the warmer she felt. She wasn't sure if it was the fire, or the power inside him, but either way, it made the going easier. As it drew nearer, she began to see distorted images, fractured glimpses of Dro'Kal's own dreams.

She felt fire and rage, heard the screams of someone she could not see, teeth sinking into flesh. Slowly, she began to see visions of him absorbing magic from one of the fonts. It was blurry, difficult to decipher what she was actually seeing. She sensed his power grow as she watched it unfold before in fractured scenes.

There were other images, too, faint glimpses of his past life. His crowning, ascending the throne, even his mother, from what Liotha could tell. She pushed past these, focusing. In order to enter his current dreams, she needed to find the source.

After being bombarded with more memories, she finally spotted it–the center of his consciousness.

As she approached it, it was unlike anything she'd seen before. A shadowy abyss, flashes of red light illuminating crimson, snake-like tendrils extending from somewhere within the void, Dro'Kal's center was more like a nightmare than a dream. When Liotha had practiced on others, it was nothing like this.

Liotha hesitated, second guessing her decision. She had no idea what kind of dark dreams lay beyond–what kind of twisted landscape she'd find on the other side.

She remembered Taura, and even Garn, their courage in the face of formidable power. This was her moment. The world needed her to succeed. She couldn't afford to be afraid.

Cautiously, she stepped inside.

CHAPTER NINE

NIGHTMARES

T he world around Liotha morphed into a twisted reality as she stepped through the portal.

All around her, there were more visions of Dro'Kal's memories, but these were unlike the ones she'd seen before. These shadows were at the core of his consciousness, raging like a torrent of corrupted versions of himself all vying for control of his mind. This dream—or more appropriately, nightmare—was so distorted she could scarcely distinguish any one thing for very long before it faded or twisted into something else entirely.

Knowing how the Dream worked, Liotha tried to steel her nerves and press on, ignoring the fleeting whispers growing in her mind. While they couldn't directly harm her, if she let them influence her thoughts, she could end up lost within the confines of Dro'Kal's mind.

Fortunately, she had a link to the outside. Tugging on it, she felt a strong pull back to Kalira. Still, she didn't want to test the limits of what that connection could sustain.

If her plan was going to work, she needed to find Dro'Kal's core manifestation within this hellish landscape. To do that, she needed to focus. Any one of these apparitions could be his true self, but if she wanted to know for sure, she needed to watch for the tells.

She'd learned to spot them when she'd practiced on volunteers the weeks prior. While in the Dream, nothing is quite as it seems. Tells, as they called them, are fragments of the dreamer's true persona shining through. They are indicators of who they are at their very core. They can be used to decipher who one truly is over how they wish the world would see them.

The only problem is, Liotha didn't really know who Dro'Kal was. She'd studied all of Mother's notes, trying her best to understand the motives and driving force behind his decisions. The notes were riddled with inconsistencies. It was as if key pieces of the puzzle were missing, linking everything together in a coherent manner. She knew Dro'Kal had not always been as he was now. Some pivotal event had changed him, but what that event was, nothing Liotha had read had given much of a clue.

Her mind replayed the visions she'd seen on her way in. There had been no indication of what might have happened–no clue that might point her in the right direction. Perhaps somewhere in here, she'd find it.

Liotha was so deep in thought she didn't notice the shadows of an enormous shape looming above her. Tripping over something on the ground and nearly falling, she slowed and glanced upwards, spotting it.

There was a long set of stairs leading up to a building that seemed somewhat familiar. As she studied its misshapen structure, it suddenly dawned on her. It was twisted, like everything else in this place, but there was no questioning, it was the palace at Dor'Dragos.

It made sense why the palace was here, but the real question was what she would find inside.

She ascended the cracked and crumbling stairs carefully, watching her footing, placing her feet in gaps where roots with thorns were not covering its surface. Even still, she nearly stumbled several times on the ascent, but eventually made it to the top, staring at the large metal doors before her. She'd seen it once before, the front doors to the palace, though it had been from a distance. As she stared at them, it felt as though the doors were staring back.

Carved on the left door were the outlines of three beings. They were tall, somewhat humanoid in nature. Their features were blurred, empty spaces where their faces should have been. Their eyes were distinct, each glowing one of the prime colors–red, blue, and yellow.

Because she'd studied all aspects of dragon society, Liotha knew these beings as the Architects–the original creators of their world. She'd seen plenty of speculative drawings of what they might have looked like, but never one quite like this.

She turned her attention to the other door. Where the left door was clearer and more concise, the right door was distorted, its images more difficult to decipher. As she studied it, she believed what she was looking at was some kind of giant creature. It was less humanoid, had less of a distinct form, more ethereal in nature. Though it was different in appearance, it had a faint resemblance to the other three on the left.

A vision flashed before Liotha, a great pair of white eyes, glowing, much like the other three, but also different. She couldn't explain it but felt immense power behind them, felt herself being pulled toward them, whispers stirring in her mind, beckoning her to join whatever malice had conjured this vision.

Liotha felt a firm tug on her tether and snapped out of her trance, the whispers vanishing as the doors faded before her and an open hallway replaced it. Shaking the darkness from her mind, she gave a gentle tug back to let Kalira know she was okay and stepped forward. As she walked past the shadowy door, she eyed it, still feeling it faintly calling to her. She hastened her steps onward, to a near run, trying to get some distance from it.

Despite the corridor first appearing quite long, she reached the end in a split second, nearly stumbling into an abyss in the center of the next room. Startled by the sudden change, she gasped and leaned backwards to avoid falling into the dark pit.

Though the dream world is merely a manifestation of thoughts and visions, the experience could be quite visceral. This nightmare version of it was even worse.

Liotha calmed herself, wrenching her gaze from the darkness below to scan the area around her. There were several passages leading off in different directions, each seemingly leading to some other place that appeared nothing like Dor'Dragos.

One of the places she recognized. It was a place she'd visited when she was a child—a land called Kalinor, the home of the Kalinari people. They were humanoid, but their ears were longer, their eyes sharper, and besides dragons, were the most in-tune with magic. Their lands were to the north, on the border of the dragon's own domain. When Liotha was young, relations with the Kalinari had been good. But it had been many years since that time, and now, Liotha presumed things were not as they once were.

Liotha turned her attention to the other hallways and the lands they led to. She saw the Duralian Mountains, a place she knew was far to the north and across the sea, home of the fierce clans of Duril. Another led to what looked like a great plain, possibly the home of the nomadic tribes of Koth, though she'd only ever seen loose paintings. Finally, the last hallway she recognized led to a desert land. By its sheer size, she assumed it could only be the Sah'naran Desert, the land of the Ashar'aran people.

She studied all four hallways again, the world seeming to spin as she did. She closed her eyes and felt, reaching out with her power, hoping one of the paths would reveal itself and lead her to where Dro'Kal's conscious was waiting. But which one would it be?

Liotha pondered each again, trying to remember Mother's notes and if any of them related to something key from Dro'Kal's past. Perhaps they were only fonts of power he'd already consumed.

It's none of them.

She opened her eyes, staring at all four paths again. She heard whispers from each, beckoning her to come. These paths would only lead her astray. But there was one path that, unlike the others, was silent. Down.

Liotha cast her gaze toward the abyss in front of her. *Could it be?*

Nothing was ever straightforward in the Dream. Sometimes the least likely of options was the correct one, though even that, too, was inconsistent. *It's worth a try.*

As she focused on it, the voices from the others paths grew louder, the wind picking up all around her, seemingly trying to push her away from the pit. Now convinced it was right, Liotha took an apprehensive step forward.

The darkness swallowed her whole as she descended into oblivion. And yet, it didn't feel like falling. She seemed to float through the air, an endless void around her, the fear suffocating but also lifting her up. She couldn't tell if it was her own fear, or Dro'Kal's.

It felt like an eternity of darkness. Her chest hurt, her lungs felt empty. She struggled to control herself, holding onto hope the darkness would end.

In the blink of an eye, Liotha found herself surrounded by light, standing in the middle of some kind of garden. Tall walls of ivy reached high above her head, closing her in. There was an open path before her, splitting off in several directions. It was the only way out.

Liotha sighed. This was the right place. She could feel it—could feel Dro'Kal's conscious somewhere within this place. The voices were gone, the wind nonexistent. She took careful steps forward until she reached bisecting paths. Four paths to choose from.

A gentle sound, barely audible, reached her ears. It sounded like weeping.

Liotha turned and followed the path the sound seemed to be coming from. It looped and split multiple times, but she kept her focus on the sound, letting it guide her steps. Several more intersections and she came out into a wide-open area, lower walls and trees in a large, circular shape. In the very center of the circle sat an enormous water fountain.

Liotha approached the fountain, noting the water was pouring over and seeping into the ground. As her eyes followed the water outward, she saw it flowing into the roots of the surrounding trees and ivy walls. She was sure she even saw the trees slowly growing as they soaked it up.

Prying her eyes from the intriguing display, she noted the crying had grown louder. Walking around the outer circle of the area to her right, she peered past the fountain, looking for its source. After a few more steps, she saw someone hunched over on the other side—someone with white hair. *Dro'Kal?*

She crept closer, trying not to alarm him. As she came up, she realized it was indeed he who was crying. And he was holding someone.

It looked like a woman, limp in his arms, golden hair and fair skin, probably a little younger than Liotha herself.

Liotha had heard rumors of several love interests when Dro'Kal was younger, but she'd never seen nor heard anything more concrete than that. But now, seeing Dro'Kal's true consciousness here, it all made so much sense. There *had* been someone from his past, and she had been the piece Liotha had missed in all of Mother's notes. Love is a powerful motivator. How could she have not seen it?

Liotha saw Dro'Kal's tears were what was filling the fountain, causing it to overflow and build the walls around this place, this barrier, protecting his deepest, darkest secret.

Focusing back on him, Liotha failed to notice one of the roots of the tree protruding out of the ground. Taking another step closer, she stumbled and let out a sharp gasp.

Dro'Kal immediately looked up in her direction, his prior blue-grey eyes, now devoid of all color, staring at her in shock. His eyes bore into her, his face contorted in confusion. It seemed he didn't recognize her.

A flash of recognition and his face lit up, his eyes turning back to blue and widening, his mouth curling in a menacing manner.

"You!" he shouted, a gust of wind swirling about at his words. "How did you get in here?" He dropped the lifeless form of the princess and stood, immediately heading Liotha's direction. The winds grew stronger.

"You cannot be here!" he shouted.

Liotha took several steps backward, tripping over more roots, which were now writhing as they ascended out of the ground beneath her feet, reaching for her ankles. She backed up further, trying to get away from them. The wind was swirling all around her now, like a violent storm had set in.

"I will destroy you, Liotha!" Dro'Kal raged, roots ripping from the ground and rushing toward her.

She turned and ran, trying to transform, instantly realizing it wouldn't be possible in this realm. And so, she sprinted toward a gap in the vine wall. As she ran, she saw it closing, more roots and vines climbing out of the ground, all of them reaching out to her as she approached.

With a burst of strength, Liotha leapt through the narrow gap, the wall closing just behind her. She caught one last glimpse of Dro'Kal approaching not far behind as she did. She stood there for a moment in an eerie silence, trying to catch her breath. For the Dream, everything still felt so surreal.

The vine wall began to slowly retract, opening the way again and a gust of wind blew through it. Liotha glanced quickly around, seeing two diverging paths on either side. With haste, she chose one and started running again. Behind her, she heard a roar. *Of course,* he *can shapeshift here.*

Liotha continued to sprint, turning down a new path at every option. She had no idea which way to go, which way was out, but she could hear Dro'Kal ripping through the vegetation behind her. At any moment, she expected him to burst through and grab her.

Another path, more running. This path was longer and headed further away from the turmoil behind her. She sprinted as fast as she could, her lungs burning. When she reached the end, she turned a corner and found herself back in an area much like where she'd first found Dro'Kal, except instead of a fountain, there was a giant hole in the ground. Confused, she hurried up to it, standing on the precipice and casting her gaze down. Water ran over her feet, falling into the hole, a mist obscuring her vision from the bottom. She glanced up, saw the vine walls were drying up and wilting, some sections already crumbled over. As another section collapsed, she saw Dro'Kal clearly. He saw her and roared, charging her way.

Liotha looked down again. It was her only real option. *It worked before...*

Taking another leap of faith, she let herself plummet down into the watery oblivion. She felt the mist brush against her body as she fell, waiting, ready to hold her breath when she finally hit the water. It never came.

A gush of wind and she found herself standing in a dimly lit room beside a large bed completely covered by a canopy. She oriented herself for a few seconds and glanced upward, seeing only a roof above her head. Peering into the darkness beyond the canopy, she tried to discern if someone was there. She heard a cough, saw the dim light of what appeared to be a pair of yellow eyes beyond.

Liotha lifted part of the canopy and immediately jumped, seeing the form of Dro'Kal lying beside the woman he was holding earlier. He didn't seem to even notice Liotha. He was simply holding the figure's hand and staring blankly at her.

As Liotha watched, she began to hear a strange noise, like a whisper. At first, it only came in hushed tones, like the incoherent babble of the wind. But gradually words formed in her head.

I can help you, the voice said. *We can save her.*

"How?" Dro'Kal said without blinking.

Power. More power than you could ever imagine. All you need to do is–

There was the sound of shattering, the ground beneath Liotha's feet becoming unstable. In a split second, the floor gave out, crumbling all around the bed. Liotha tried to grab hold of the bed, but it happened too fast. She was falling again, looking up at the scene still suspended in the air above her. Everywhere below her was a burning wasteland, littered with ruins and fire. She continued to fall straight toward it.

"There you are!" came Dro'Kal's voice above her, roaring with an insatiable rage.

Liotha turned and saw he was flying straight toward her as she fell. Turning away, looking for some way to escape, she saw, far in the distance, the landscape change. It was dark and shadowed, devoid of the devastation around her now. *The edge of his consciousness?*

Liotha braced herself for impact with the ground. As she landed, she rolled and came up to her feet, surprised at how easy the maneuver had been. She whipped around and jumped, just in time for Dro'Kal to barrel into the ground next to her, his wings smashing into her and sending her flying and tumbling through sand.

This time, the impact of the ground sent an intense pain through her core. She spat out sand, wiped her face, and looked up to see Dro'Kal recovering, turning her direction and roaring again.

Liotha jumped up and began sprinting toward the void beyond the sands. It seemed closer now, though she didn't think she'd been knocked that far. Either way, it was still going to be hard to outrun Dro'Kal.

She heard him lifting off, the wind from his wings creating a violent sandstorm rushing toward her. She ran harder–harder than she'd ever run in her life. The sand whipped around her, pelting her face. She tried to keep her mouth closed, though she was desperate for air.

She drew closer to the edge but could sense Dro'Kal closing in through the sandstorm as it overtook her. She felt the power surging in his chest, knew what he was about to do.

With every step, her heart beat faster. She felt her strength slowly draining but pushed herself even harder anyways. Thirty paces. Twenty. Ten.

Dro'Kal roared as he let loose an intense wave of electricity. Liotha felt it singe her skin as she dove through the darkness beyond.

The world around her turned silent, save for the muffled sound of the lighting slamming against the invisible wall behind her. She turned and watched it, stunned at what she was seeing. The lightning just... stopped. The sands raging just beyond swirled about violently, but not a single grain passed through.

A few seconds later, she saw the raging form of Dro'Kal barreling straight toward her out of the sandstorm. She put her hands up in a kneejerk reaction, shielding herself.

She heard a thud and a grunt, putting her arms down and looking at his humanoid form lying on the ground. She took a few steps back, trying to shift herself again. *Neither of us can transform here?*

As Dro'Kal stirred, Liotha glanced all around at this new world she found herself in. Finally, they were out of his consciousness. That was good in some ways, but she didn't know what to expect out here.

No matter, now she needed to lead him away. As Dro'Kal pushed himself up, she ran. She didn't know how far she needed to go, but it didn't matter. She was so close to achieving her goal now. All she had to do was keep running.

She heard Dro'Kal behind her shouting, frustration in realizing he could no longer shift. Liotha just focused on the world around her. It was a woods of some sort, dark and foreboding. The space between, where consciousness ended and the true Dream began. Though she was in uncharted territory, she hoped the worst was behind. The woods would offer plenty of cover. Plus, it should be easier to lose Dro'Kal. However, she didn't want him to lose sight of her just yet. They needed to get further inside.

Making sure she didn't stray too far ahead, Liotha slowed her pace a bit, ensuring she let herself be seen from time to time so that Dro'Kal kept pursuing her. She could hear his breathing echoing through the trees, heard his growls in frustration, and every so often he shouted in rage at her, coaxing her to come and face him. Her plan was working flawlessly. That is, until she started to feel her own mind slipping.

At first, it was subtle, glimpsing shadows moving amongst the trees. She didn't think much of it at first because that's how the Dream works. Everything you see is never quite as it should be. Shadows moving on their own was normal. But the shadows grew and eventually wore faces, some of them seeming familiar. She heard their cries, heard their anguish. She saw faces she recognized, beckoning her to follow. She saw others she didn't know, urging her to abandon her task and take a rest. And there were others still, darker, more menacing, simply smiling at her.

That's when Liotha knew it had been too long. Time passes differently in the Dream, so what felt like minutes here could be hours or even days on the outside, or vice versa. She had no way of knowing how long she had been in the Dream, or how long she had been running. It was worrying, as her own mind could get lost in this forsaken place. Luckily, she had an anchor in the real world. She felt it still, though it was growing thin. She was running out of time.

She didn't know if she was far enough away for Dro'Kal to not find his way back. She still heard him, but he sounded distant, his own confusion seeming to have set in. She couldn't tell which direction he was anymore.

It was time to go. Hopefully, Dro'Kal was deep enough that their plan would succeed, but Liotha couldn't last much longer, or she'd be trapped along with him.

Liotha could feel her connection to Kalira, though it was weak. With all her might, she pulled on the tether. At first, nothing happened, but after several seconds, she felt her feet lift off the ground, felt herself flung through the void, climbing toward the stars above. She saw what appeared to be Dro'Kal's consciousness far off in the distance, appearing like just another star in the void beyond. Somehow, they'd traveled much further than she'd thought. *Hopefully, it's enough.*

The tether pulled Liotha through darkness for a short while before the stars ahead of her grew in size, each one an image of some far-off dreamer's memories. They were others' realms of consciousness. She'd read about it in the books, but this was her first time seeing it for what it was. It was quite beautiful, though she knew the beauty was only an allure.

Liotha felt an odd sensation and turned, noticing a portion of the sky that was pure darkness, devoid of stars. The darkness took form, almost like the creature she'd seen on the door of the palace.

Just as Liotha noticed it, she felt another strong tug on her tether. She gazed up, noticing one of the conscious realms looming above. It was her own, memories of events both recent and long ago flashing in front of her eyes. She was moving quickly toward it now, at an almost dizzying pace.

There was a sharp sense of fear that could be felt through the tether, followed by one last strong tug. And then, nothing.

Liotha's speed slowly declined until she came to a crawl. She was close now, floating maybe a hundred or so feet from returning to her body. But try as she might, she could scarcely move, and for whatever reason, the tether with Kalira was gone. Something was wrong. *Has Dro'Kal already awoken?*

Liotha desperately tried to move forward, but it was like swimming in an ocean with no water. There was nothing to grab onto, nothing to push off of. She was stuck, the edges of her own mind caving in again with the tether cut off. Shadows swirled around her, like fingers grasping at her consciousness. There was nothing below anymore. The ground was gone. All that remained was the light of her mind above and the endless void below.

I can help you, she heard a voice say—the same voice she'd heard speaking to Dro'Kal at the bedside. *He was weak, but you... you could be so much more.*

Liotha tried to push the voice out. She did not know who—or what—it was. It could be just the Dream playing tricks on her. Whatever it was, she couldn't let it affect her, otherwise she would be lost forever. But she also needed to figure out how to get moving, or else it would all be in vain.

Stay here in the Dream. There's nothing for you out there...

"Oh, but there is," Liotha said aloud. Whether the voice was real or imagined, she needed to drive it out of her thoughts. But it had also reminded her of something. The magic in her belly—her children.

She hadn't realized it before, but she felt it now, their presence. Their consciousness was their own, and while it was weaker than Kalira's, it could act as a tether. Liotha reached out, sensing them—their warmth, the magic within them.

"There you are," she said aloud.

She pulled on it gently, moving slightly forward. It worked!

She continued to pull slowly, not knowing how fragile it was. Gradually, she made her way closer to her consciousness—closer to her body and her children.

She turned around, saw the darkness from before, part of it reaching out toward her.

They are weak. They may not survive. I can give you the power to save them.

Liotha paused. Was this creature of shadow talking about her children? In her moment of hesitation, the darkness drew closer.

Liotha shook her head, trying desperately to keep herself from succumbing to this strange evil. Though she had to admit, its allure was strong, tempting. What if they *were* dying? Everything she'd gone through, everything she'd done would be for nothing.

Just as Liotha felt herself losing control, she felt a slight tug on her tether. It was a momentary second for her mind to clear, for her to remember her children.

No. Whatever or whoever this shadow was, it was lying. She couldn't trust it.

Liotha tugged back. In a brilliant flash of light, she breached her own mind. She felt a tingle run down her spine as everything went black for a few seconds. And then she opened her eyes.

She was back in the real world, though everything was a bit blurry. Her eyes came into focus as she stared at her own hands in front of her. Turning to her side, she noticed Kalira lying limp beside her, a pool of blood surrounding her body.

Liotha sat up, trying to process what she was seeing. Holding her breath, she searched for the others. She saw Hiroma, her body the same. *Taura?*

Hearing a grunt, she turned and saw a man standing over Taura, a spear pressed into her back, her face covered in splatters of blood. Their eyes locked for a moment as Taura held her gaze and smiled.

You made it. I did my job. Tell Mother—

With a twist, the spear shaft pierced Taura's back, her eyes growing wide for several seconds before the light slowly faded from them. Liotha flinched, trying to stand and run to her friend. She felt a prick on the back of her neck and froze, saw others approach her sides, spears raised. From within the shadows in front of her, out stepped Garn.

"You betrayed us, dragon," Garn said, his tone cold and flat. "I put my own and the lives of my men at stake to help you end this bastard," he continued, his eyes flicking to Dro'Kal's body. "I lost twelve men today because of you. That is why *your* friends are dead, though it hardly seems even just yet."

Liotha swallowed, looking around at the corpses of her companions.

"Now, before I decide what to do with you, you're going to tell me what the hell's so special about this wyrm of yours, and what exactly you were doing just now."

She couldn't. If Garn knew the truth, there was no telling what he would do. Whatever it was, it would almost certainly ruin everything. The only chance Liotha had was to get Dro'Kal's body and get away. But Garn and his surviving companions had proven their resolve, and the spear point in the back of her head was not something she could underestimate.

"Answer my question, dragon," Garn said, raising his voice. Liotha thought she saw a flicker of light in his eyes.

She'd escaped the nightmares only to wake up in a new one, this one even worse than the last. If she didn't think fast, there might be no escaping this one.

CHAPTER TEN

ESCAPE

Liotha's eyes scanned Garn's companions within her view. They all stared at her with cold eyes, their intent clear in their expressions. Liotha turned her attention back to Garn.

"Like I told you before, he has been consuming the world's magic. You saw the power he wielded. It cannot continue."

"Then let us end him now and be done with it," Garn said, walking toward Dro'Kal's body.

"No!" Liotha spat, reaching out her hand.

Garn paused, looking back at her in an assessing gaze.

"What aren't you telling me?" he asked, his eyes narrowing.

Liotha's mind raced once again. She used her senses to reach out to the minds of Garn's men. Most were overridden with malice, their thoughts too clouded for her to perceive anything but darkness. But there was one. His thoughts seemed more conflicted than the rest. As she tried to discern who it was, his thoughts came from behind her. It was the one holding the spear to her neck. She noticed now the very slight tremble in his grip at the other end of the spear. *He's nervous. Good.*

"Well?" Garn asked louder, stepping toward her.

"We can't kill him. Not yet. We don't know what might happen if we do."

"What do you mean?" Garn asked, looking at Dro'Kal's limp form. "And what happens if he wakes up? I don't want to fight this bastard again."

"He won't," Liotha said, trying to sound sure, though the thought had crossed her mind as a possibility.

She reached out, feeling for the man holding the spear, her thoughts pressing into his. *She's lying. He could wake at any moment.*

She felt the tip of the spear tremble a little more. She sensed further doubt, used the opening to crawl deeper into his mind.

Ready your spear, she commanded. She felt the tip of the spear pull back slightly. Liotha turned her attention to the body of Hiroma. Her heart dipped seeing her open eyes amidst the bloody snow, but even in death, the dragoness gave her an idea. Liotha tried to remember the lessons with Hiroma the weeks prior to leaving. She'd learned a few deception skills from the dragoness. Perhaps one of them would work on the man behind her.

Reaching through her connection with him, she attempted to persuade him he was seeing Dro'Kal stir. After a handful of seconds, it seemed to not be working.

"What are you doing?" Garn asked, stepping toward her.

Liotha tried again, pushing harder, trying to not let it show in her features.

"Stop," Garn shouted, raising his spear toward her. Several of the others around her moved closer. "I said–"

"He's moving," the man behind Liotha said. She felt him raise his spear and point it toward Dro'Kal. Everyone's eyes followed.

Not wasting a second, Liotha spun, growing in size, spreading her wings and knocking away all those around her. It created a moment of chaos, and she seized it.

With only a few seconds to react, Liotha dove straight toward Garn, who was alone for the moment. Faster than she could track him, he dodged her attack and rolled to the side and underneath her. Her plan wasn't to fight, so she kept moving. As she charged toward Dro'Kal's body, she felt a sharp sting in her side. Ignoring it, she continued several more paces, placed one her claws around Dro'Kal's body and grabbed him, using her other leg to push herself upward into the air.

She heard shouts behind her as she soared upward and above the trees, only glancing back once she felt she'd made it out of range of their spear throws. They were all shouting, their spears poised to throw. Garn waved for them to stop. He stood there, calm and collected, just staring at her. Liotha was relieved to leave them behind her but couldn't shake the gnawing feeling in the back of her mind that, to end one monster, she'd created another of near equal.

Shaking her head, Liotha soared higher. Garn and his men had somehow tracked them the first time. She couldn't afford to let that happen again. She glanced down to the body of Dro'Kal still clutched in her claw. *One monster at a time.*

She veered southward just over the next hill and began her flight toward home. As her pulse slowed and her nerves calmed, she started to notice a sharp pain in her leg. Craning her neck to see what the cause was, she noticed a large gash along her right leg, as well as a small cut in her wing. The wing wasn't bleeding much, but blood still flowed from the other wound. Garn had landed a strike as she'd escaped.

After realizing the extent of the damage, she began to feel the weakness seeping into her muscles. The sharp pain bit at her leg, and she could feel her grip on Dro'Kal weakening. She had hoped to get much more distance from the humans before landing, but she wasn't sure how far she'd be able to make it with the wound still seeping.

She scanned the surrounding hills and mountains for a safe place to land. If she was lucky, she could land, patch herself up, and keep going. As she continued to look, she felt herself slowly dropping lower. Her muscles were giving out, and at any moment, she felt she might lose her power to maintain her dragon form.

Liotha dipped quickly, spotting a small clearing of trees up ahead at the base of the next mountain. It was open and exposed, but it would have to do.

She found it was getting harder and harder to focus, her vision beginning to get cloudy, her head feeling a bit light. Her depth perception wavered in and out, and before she knew it, she was ploughing headfirst into a heavy, snowy bank. Fortunately, the snow was deep enough she didn't hurt herself on the landing, though she had to dig herself out, careful of Dro'Kal's body, which had gotten buried momentarily.

Once they were both uncovered, Liotha, still clinging to her dragon skin, checked herself over. She was still bleeding from her leg, though it was steadily slowing. She scanned the area for any potential cover, spotting only the tree line a little way back. As her only option for the moment, she carefully grabbed Dro'Kal in her jaws and moved to the cover of the trees. Unable to maintain her form any longer, Liotha plopped down in the snow beside Dro'Kal's still body and lay there for several minutes.

After a momentary rest, she sat up and examined her leg. It was a nasty gash. Her adrenaline must have kept her from realizing how bad it had actually been in the moment. She glanced up and scanned the area, noticing the bloody trail she'd left in the snow. If the humans did follow her, they might be able to follow the trail of blood she'd undoubtedly left through the mountains. They'd already tracked her down once, and that was across a much further distance. She was too weak to fly anymore. She needed to find somewhere to hide.

Liotha ripped off a small piece of her tunic and wrapped it around her wound. It would help temporarily, but she needed to rest and keep it elevated to get it to stop fully.

Deciding to leave Dro'Kal in the snow for the moment, she set out to check the local area for somewhere better to hide. Going one direction, she followed the tree line, scanning the woods and the steep incline to her right. Perhaps she could find an outcropping of rocks or even a cave, if lucky, where she could clean up and get a fire going. She couldn't have Dro'Kal freezing to death, either.

When she'd gone several hundred feet the one direction and found nothing, she doubled back and, after checking on Dro'Kal, checked the other direction.

As she limped along, nothing stood out to her as a reasonable place to hide. Just as she was about to give up and turn back, she noticed the ground dipped up ahead, a large section of the mountain looking like it had caved in. Cresting the edge of the small ridge, she peered down into a narrow ravine running straight into an opening in the side of the mountain. Liotha sighed in relief. Her luck, it seemed, wasn't completely out, though she had no idea what the cave might hold.

It took her a short while to get back to Dro'Kal, and with her waning strength, she hoisted him on her back. Getting back to the cave was much slower, but after a short while she managed to climb the rim again. Getting down, however, was going to be tricky. There was less snow here but only because it was steeper and rockier.

Liotha made it a short way down before feeling the rocks crumble beneath her feet, causing her to slip. She winced in pain, nearly dropping Dro'Kal. Looking down, she saw a fresh scratch on her already battered leg.

"Curse the gods," she said, looking to the sky. "Curse these blasted mountains."

Liotha propped herself up steadily, wincing from all the pain. Only a short way further and she would be down the hill. Then, it was a straight shot to the cave.

Fortunately, she made it down the rest of the way without slipping. Steadying herself, she waited for her head to stop spinning. The blood loss was getting to her.

Inside, the cave was larger than it had first appeared. Even in her dragon form, she could've easily fit inside. Even flew, perhaps, if she wasn't on the verge of passing out. As she entered the mouth of the cave, the air felt slightly warmer. It was more humid, too.

It took a few seconds for her eyes to adjust to the darkness, but fortunately her dragon eyesight made seeing in the dark a quick adjustment. At least, if Garn did catch up to her, that was one advantage she had down here over them.

The cave entrance slowly expanded as Liotha progressed deeper inside. The air steadily grew warmer, which was a curious phenomenon considering the mountains outside were always covered in snow and ice year-round. If such was the case down here, that could only mean one thing—this was much more than a small cave. To have a source of heat, it must be quite extensive.

As Liotha predicted, after several more twists and turns through the cavern, it opened up into a much wider area. Though her eyesight let her see well enough, she still couldn't see the other end. There were large pillars throughout the massive area, and elevated areas well above her head, while other areas descended deeper below. But even beyond the sheer size of the place, it was the slight echo of dripping water that drew Liotha's attention.

After ascending a nearby rocky area, she came into view of a small, underground lake. It wasn't much bigger than the small lakes back home, but considering its location, its size was still rather impressive. The lake was calm and still, other than the occasional drip, sending barely noticeable ripples across the glassy surface.

Glancing up, Liotha spotted several cracks along the ceiling of the cave. Some of them were letting a faint amount of light through. With the light, she tried to find a way down to the water's edge. Her leg was throbbing, and the warm, assumedly clear water should do nicely to clean and dress herself. Tightening her grip on Dro'Kal, she descended the slope and carefully made her way to the lake.

Setting Dro'Kal down gently, quickly looking over him for any major injuries, of which there appeared none, she sat down and began unwrapping her makeshift bandage from earlier. She winced as the last blood-soaked layers of cloth separated from her skin. The bleeding was better now, probably thanks to the cold, but the wound definitely needed cleaning. She slid her foot into the water. It was warmer than she'd expected, but it made sense. It must be why the cavern was so warm and humid.

It felt good as she dipped the rest of her leg in, slowly letting all the blood and filth wash off. Moving her hands down into the water, she gently scrubbed her leg clean. She winced again as her fingers crossed over the wounds.

After a few more splashes of water, she pulled her leg up and examined it. The cut was deep, and even now fresh blood was slowly seeping from it, but it had slowed enough to not be of so much concern. Still, she needed to rewrap it to ensure it stopped entirely. Glancing sideways toward Dro'Kal, she had an idea.

Doesn't need all his clothes, she thought, reaching down and pulling his undershirt out from beneath his jerkin. It was full of ruffles, so there was enough fabric to cover her wound. Once she had a solid strip separated, she dipped it in the water, cleaning it as much as she could.

Wringing it out as much as possible, she carefully wrapped her leg, taking her time this time to ensure a proper bandage. Just as she was finishing securing the knots, a sound caught her ear. She stopped and listened, holding her breath. She heard a slight shuffling noise, accompanied by the distinct sound of metal grating against metal. A deep dread came over her. *Already?*

Liotha stood and grabbed Dro'Kal, throwing him back over her shoulder. Her energy was still low, but she felt a little less woozy after cleaning and dressing her wound. The warmth helped, too.

As silently as she could manage, Liotha crept deeper into the cave. Following the shoreline until she came to one of the giant pillars, she stepped behind it to take a break and see if you could spot her pursuers. Holding her hand up, she could tell her eyes had a faint glow. Hopefully, they wouldn't get her spotted.

Peering around the edge, she saw the outlines of several men standing by the water. One of them was hunched down, holding something in his hand. Her discarded wraps. *Damnit. How could I have been so stupid.*

The one holding the wraps glanced up, scanning the edge of the lake. She could see clearly now it was Garn. And moreover, his eyes had a dim glow, just like hers. *Is it possible?*

His eyes moved across where Liotha was hiding and she quickly ducked back behind the pillar, unsure whether he'd seen her or not. She steadied her breath, scanning her own side of the cave for where to go next. Even if he hadn't seen her, it wouldn't be long before they found her trail.

She spotted what looked like a dark passage between several more pillars. It was her best bet. She crept toward it, with haste now, expecting to be ambushed at any minute. Making it safely there, she stole a glance backward. She couldn't see them, but still heard their sounds as if they'd drawn closer.

The cave before her was smaller than the one she'd entered before. Darker, too. Darker was good for her, but Garn, if his eyes glowed as hers did, it was possible he had some manner of vision in the darkness. That was not good.

Hearing the sounds growing closer, and with no other immediate options, Liotha moved into the tunnel. Once she rounded a curve in the cave, she quickened her pace even further, hoping the tunnel would mask any sounds she might make. Liotha had to assume that if these humans had some of her abilities, it was possible they might have others, too. It seemed she'd created something much worse than she'd originally anticipated.

The cave wound this way and that for some time. Every so often, Liotha would pause and calm her breathing to listen. For a time, she heard no sounds of pursuit. But after a short while, she began to hear the distinct sounds of her hunters in pursuit. It was hard to tell how far behind they were, but it was obvious they were catching up.

The cave suddenly split, branching in two directions. As Liotha debated which way to go, she heard a whizzing noise, stepping to the side just in time for something to swoosh past her, slicing a piece of flesh along her side as it embedded into the nearby wall. She gasped in pain but moved into a full sprint down the direction she was already facing. There was no more time for choices.

She felt fresh blood soaking her side, the pain growing in waves, but she had no time to stop and worry about it. Liotha ran as fast as she could, hearing shouting and metal clanking now that her hunters were in hot pursuit.

Liotha had no idea how she was going to get out of this one. The men were stronger and more resilient than she'd given them credit. It was only a matter of time before they caught her.

As Liotha began to feel herself slowing, she stumbled out into another large, open cavern. This one wasn't as large as the first, but her sounds echoed more here for some reason. As she kept sprinting, moving slightly up in elevation, trying to figure out why, she finally understood.

There was a large gap in the floor up ahead, a crevice going down deeper into the earth. She slowed to a stop as she approached the ledge, gazing down into a darkness even Liotha's eyes could not pierce.

The sound of pursuit behind her, Liotha spun to see the men emerging from the smaller cave. They spotted her instantly. All their eyes now glowed dimly as Garn's did.

"There you are, dragon. Good thing I gave you that," Garn said, glancing down toward her bandaged leg. "Wasn't hard to follow the trail of blood, especially with our new gifts. This power you've given us..." he said with a devious grin. "This truly is worth the price we paid. It seems even you underestimated its potential."

Liotha stepped back toward the ledge, knocking several pebbles down into the void below. She looked back, eyeing it momentarily.

"You've got nowhere to run, now. Time to hand over your wyrm and face the inevitable."

Liotha eyes shifted sideways. She had no idea if she had the strength, but it was her only chance. But before she faced her possible end, she needed to address her demons.

"I am sorry," Liotha said, trying to stand tall in the face of Garn's advance.

"Sorry? I think we're a little past that now" Garn said, frowning.

"Not sorry about that," Liotha said. "You were always meant to be pawns. I came to terms with that long before I met you. No, I am sorry that I offered you a taste of something beyond your comprehension. I am sorry I gave you something the world will covet for years to come. I am sorry I replaced one monster with another."

"Hah," Garn chuckled, followed by snickering from several of the others. "Of course you're sorry. You played your cards, and you lost. It's not my fault we can play the same cards now, and it's time to pay up." Garn inched closer with every word.

"Ah, but that's where you're wrong, dragon-killer. You have my sight; I can see it in your eyes. You are strong and resilient—more so than I expected. But there is one last card I can play that you never will."

Liotha glanced back again. She saw Garn notice the ravine now, his eyes flashing wide in realization of her words.

"No!" he said at the same instant she threw Dro'Kal back over her shoulder, spinning as quickly as she could and attempting to shift into her dragon form. She felt her energy cut short, her arms and legs flailing as she fell into the darkness after Dro'Kal. She heard the swish of a spear being thrown in the dark, narrowly missing her, and heard shouts from Garn and the men above.

Liotha felt like she was in a dream—flashbacks of Dro'Kal's nightmares echoing through her mind. Except this wasn't a dream. There would be no soft landing at the bottom of this darkness. But she was so weak now, her strength sapped from her. She didn't think she would be able to save herself.

She thought of how far she'd come, how so much had happened in so little time. She thought of Kalira and Hiroma, the sacrifices they'd made to help her. She thought of Taura, who'd given her life to protect Liotha to the very end. She thought of Mother and all she'd done to help Liotha become more than she'd ever have become on her own. She thought of Kel'ana and the sacrifice she'd made to see the world made better. She thought of her children, their magic so faint in her belly now she could scarcely tell if they were even still there.

It couldn't have all happened, just to end like this, could it? Defeated by the monsters she herself had created. Liotha remembered Mother Ere'daina's story of Zareena.

No.

At that moment, something stirred within Liotha—the raw power she'd tapped into only once before, albeit briefly, when Hel'aren had attacked her. She would not allow her monsters to defeat her. She would not become another Zareena.

Liotha's eyes flashed a brilliant violet, illuminating the darkness around her. As they did, she caught a glimpse of Dro'Kal's lifeless body below her. She swung her arms out, her wings spreading wide as she did. Transforming all the way, she brought her claws out before her and snatched Dro'Kal in her clutches.

Pressing down with her wings with several strong thrusts, she slowed herself until she was hovering in the darkness. She glanced down, the darkness seeming to continue forever. Glancing back up, she could scarcely see traces of light above.

With this new vigor, she might stand a chance against them. They needed to be dealt with, but she didn't know how long this surge of power would last. It might not be worth the risk.

She pondered her two options. She could see how far the darkness would take her, or rise up and face the monsters above.

Liotha chose darkness.

CHAPTER ELEVEN

QUEEN

L iotha stood quietly in a large antechamber, a growing crowd gathering just beyond the large doors in front of her. She fidgeted in her form-fitting dress, feeling a bit awkward. The dress was stunning, probably a hundred times more expensive than anything she'd ever owned. She should have been thrilled, but all she felt was guilt.

If only Kel'ana could see me now. She would've fawned over the luxurious dress.

Mother told her if she was going to be Queen, she needed to look the part.

Glancing around at the red and white walls surrounding her, their surfaces polished and pristine, a few scattered paintings of places she'd never been and dragons she did not know, she felt nearly as empty as the room itself. It was big, though—that was for sure. *Not quite the move I wished for all those days ago...*

It had been about half a cycle since she'd returned to Dor'Dragos and hailed as a hero. Not a day had gone by where she'd actually felt like one. Dro'Kal was no longer a threat, his body hidden where no one would ever find him, but the world continued to decline, much of its magic still held captive within his body. With Hiroma and Kalira gone, she'd had no option but to continue to search for ways to transfer his magic back on her own. Liotha had consorted with many versed in the ways of transfer magic, but none of them offered the skill she needed. She even attempted to solicit Hiroma's mother for help, but the dragoness would have nothing to do with her. Liotha didn't blame her.

Liotha had stayed up late many nights on her own, delving into the ancient magics even deeper, but it was to no avail. She'd found pieces of the puzzle, but so far, there were still too many missing pieces. Nothing like this had ever happened before. Still, she was determined to eventually set things right. Which was, in part, why she'd been dreading this day for many moons.

Liotha was to be crowned the first Queenmother of the dragon empire—a privilege no dragoness had ever held since the dawn of time. It was Mother Ere'daina's idea from the start. Liotha always presumed Mother had wanted the station for herself, but it seemed it had always been Liotha who she'd intended to sit in Dro'Kal's seat once he was gone. Though, as of yet, Mother had been resistant to say specifically why.

"You look extravagant," came a familiar voice from behind. "Always knew you were meant for this."

Liotha's eyes glanced sideways as Mother came up beside her.

"And did it ever occur to you this might not be the life *I* wanted?" Liotha asked, keeping her eyes locked on the large set of doors ahead of her.

"We must all make sacrifices if we are to see the world change."

"Sacrifices... I know you came to terms with your demons long ago, Mother. But for me, I'm still wrestling with mine. And right now, I'm not so sure I'm winning."

"It gets easier with time," Mother said, turning to face Liotha with a smile. "You're strong. You will overcome them."

"That's the thing, though. I'm not sure I want to. I've done things–terrible things, and all for what? To sit on a throne I never wanted? To replace one monster with another? And we've still yet to achieve our ultimate goal."

"Dro'Kal is no more. That was our goal. The rest are unfortunate side effects. One cannot predict all possible outcomes."

"The goal was to heal the wounds of this world, and you know as well as I do those wounds run deep. With so much magic ripped from the leylines, there's no telling what will happen. Despite our best efforts, the other races continue to suffer."

"It is true, yes, wounds will forever leave scars. But the world can come to terms with them, just as you have come to term with yours." Mother nodded to Liotha, gazing past the mask she still wore and looking deep into her eyes.

Liotha reached up to her mask, almost forgetting it was there. She'd grown so accustomed to it, almost forgetting it was there entirely at times. *Have I come to terms with it? Or have I just grown used to hiding behind it?*

"Scars are one thing," Liotha said, pushing her thoughts aside. "But magic? That is something else entirely. I do not know if the world can heal from such wounds."

"Well, from what I understand, you're still working on that."

"I'm trying, but I'm getting nowhere. I'm starting to think it's not possible."

"I'm sure you'll find a way." There was a long pause before Mother spoke again. "You still never told me where you hid him."

"And I told you that I'm not going to. I cannot risk that information falling into the wrong hands. He still has allies hiding in the shadows of this city. I won't risk any chance at them catching wind of his whereabouts."

"I understand the need to keep secrets better than anyone. Though I do not agree with your decision, I respect your intentions."

Liotha dipped her head to Mother just as she heard the voice of the announcer on the other side of the door. The ceremony had officially begun, though it would be a few minutes before the doors opened and Liotha would reveal herself. *Am I really about to do this?*

"I'm not sure I'm ready for this," Liotha said.

"No one is ever truly ready to lead. You will make mistakes, and you will learn."

"I've already made too many mistakes. There must be more qualified candidates. You still never told me why you didn't want to be Queen."

Mother's face softened. The last time Liotha asked, Mother changed the topic, insisting Liotha was who it needed to be. But now, as she gazed apathetically into Liotha's eyes, it seemed she might finally answer truthfully.

"It could never be me, Liotha. I can be a Scion, yes, but never Queen. I have made too many enemies, and my ascension would only cause discord amongst the Houses. Besides, you've made far fewer mistakes than I have. I told you my story before. My heart is hard, my mind is... not what it used to be. But you—you are still pure. You may not think it, but I see it, even now in your questioning. You are the right one for this honor."

"But that's just it, I'm not. The things I've done to get here, the ones I've left behind, who's blood is on my hands—I can't possibly be fit for Queen."

"Liotha," Mother said, taking both of Liotha's hands in her own. "None of that blood is on you. I am the one who orchestrated all of this. I have taken their blood on my hands so you don't have to. You must see it."

"What do you mean? I was the one who—"

"I recruited Kalira and Hiroma to assist you. You only chose them because I brought them to you."

Liotha processed Mother's words. It was true, from a certain point of view.

"I ordered Taura to accompany you. You needed protection. Your life was more valuable than hers. She gave her life to keep yours safe by my command."

Though it pained Liotha to think Taura had only acted on Mother's orders, it made sense. Taura had always been completely loyal to Mother.

"But what of Hel'aren? I just let them—"

"The humans killed him, not you."

"Yes, but I—"

"He was only there that day because I planted the information in Dro'Kal's ear through him."

"What? What do you mean?" Liotha asked, her eyes scrutinizing the dragoness's words.

"He wanted so desperately to prove his loyalty, he was easily swayed to believe our lie. It was his lips that brought the discovery of the false leyline to the Wyrmlord's inner circle. Even earned him a place on the excursion, apparently, though I didn't anticipate that."

Part of Liotha wanted to cry. She'd gotten over the death of her mate some time ago, but a wave of fresh thoughts washed over her now. Had it really been Mother all along?

"And what of Kel'ana. Surely you—" Liotha stopped, thinking back to the events of that day in the Council chamber. "Did you...?"

Mother's expression shifted, her eyes dodging away, a hint of red appearing in her cheeks for the first time. Mother had always been hard to read, but at the mention of Kel'ana, it was apparent she'd struck a nerve.

"You didn't stop them. But why? You never told me how they found out about Kel'ana."

"I– I am sorry, Liotha. I told you. I have done many things, many awful things. What happened to Kel'ana was never my intention. It broke my heart."

"What did you do?" Liotha asked, her heart racing. A minute ago, she was nearly ready to cry, now she felt a sudden anger growing within her. Kel'ana had been her closest friend, and all those who'd died, probably the most innocent.

"I couldn't let them dig too deeply. I couldn't let them discover you. They needed someone to punish, and..." Mother paused, seemingly genuine in her sorrow. "It wasn't supposed to be her, but I had no choice."

"No choice?" Liotha said, raising her voice. "There's always a choice. She was my best friend, and you led her straight to her slaughter–for me, someone you hardly knew at the time. You couldn't have known I would even succeed, let alone accept the responsibility."

Liotha turned away from Mother, trying to decide her next move. She wanted to turn around and wrap her hands around the Scion's throat. She wanted to dig her claws into her chest and wrench her cold, dark heart from her body. Of all the monsters Liotha had faced, perhaps the greatest one had been right in front of her all along.

"And what of the missing younglings? I suppose that was you, too?" Liotha raised her voice, turning back to Mother, though she didn't really expect it to be true.

"We needed to convince the families to join our cause. Dro'Kal's followers put up quite the fight. We needed more support. I thought if I could convince them he had a hand in it–"

"I can't believe you," Liotha fumed. "Even the children. All this time, how could I not have seen it? Was it worth it? You can't possibly tell me it was worth it–that we're standing here today and all of them are dead just to see your puppet ascend to the throne."

"You are not a puppet, Liotha. You must believe I had the best of intentions. For the greater good." Liotha heard the desperation in Mother's voice.

The words of the announcer on the other side of the door caught her ear. She remembered them from their rehearsal. It was nearly time. There was no way she could go on with this... not now. Not after all that had just been revealed.

"I can't–"

"They are not all dead," Mother said, cutting Liotha off.

"What? Who's not dead?"

"The younglings. At least, I presume they are not dead."

"What did you do with them?" Liotha asked, her eyes narrowing as she stepped closer to Mother.

"They are with the humans."

Liotha's jaw dropped.

"You gave them to the humans? Why? Did you not hear anything I told about their strength?"

"It was before–before I knew how effective your method was. I swear it."

"Why would you give them the younglings in the first place?"

"They needed blood. Plus, it was a contingency–in case your plan failed. With a steady supply of blood, they could grow stronger, perhaps even strong enough to defeat Dro'Kal should our original plan fail."

"I can't believe this..." Liotha trailed off, unsure of exactly what to say.

As she thought, the doors began to open, the announcer hailing the new queen to emerge. Liotha gazed out of the dark room into the large auditorium beyond.

"I can't do this. I can't be Queen. I need to figure out how to fix this mess."

"You can, and you must. Perhaps we *can* fix this, but not without you taking the throne."

"No more tricks, no more lies. Tell them it's off." Liotha turned and began walking away from Mother and the light beyond the door.

"If we do that," Mother said, "who knows what will happen. If the seat of power lies vacant, others will arise to challenge it. And if that happens, it could mean civil war, and then you will never get the support you need to try and make things right. We've already come all this way. You must see this is the only option."

Liotha stopped and glanced backward. She wanted to argue and continue walking away, but Mother's words rang true in her heart. She wasn't sure if she believed all of what the Scion was saying, but it made sense. There were plenty who would vie for the throne should she decline. They'd had a hard enough time convincing the Council and the rest of the Houses that change was necessary. The city was still in turmoil with the news of its new Queen, though they'd quelled most of the worst troublemakers.

"If what you say is true, and perhaps it is," Liotha said, turning around, "then I may have no choice–at least, not in becoming Queen. But I will not have anyone else's blood on my hands. That is a choice I *do* have. *I* will set things right. *I* will fix whatever evil can yet be undone. And *you* will do all you can to aid me. And then, once all is right, you will account for your sins, Scion."

Liotha removed her mask and shoved it in Mother's chest with her last words, glaring at the Scion with her scarred face.

As Mother glanced down at the mask in her hands, Liotha headed through the doors, leaving the Scion alone in the dark room. Her heart raced as she stepped out into the light, the roaring cheer of the thousands who'd flocked there to see her crowning stifling the raging thoughts flowing through her head.

This was the dawn of a new day, not only for her, but for the beginning of change within the world. Liotha would suffer monsters no more, nor would she allow herself to become the very thing she fought to destroy.

Today, she walked in darkness no longer.

Chapter Twelve

Hope

As she sat in the darkness of her private quarters in the palace, Liotha contemplated all the words she'd just written on the piece of paper sitting on the desk in front of her. All that had been weighing on her conscious was all there, inscribed in ink, a true retelling for those who would eventually read it.

Liotha needed future queens to know the road she'd taken. She needed them to do better—to be better.

Liotha had tried to be a good queen, tried to instigate change. It was possible, and things were already changing for the better. And there were signs things could yet improve further. She'd convinced a great many dragons, both male and female, to take her side. She had allies she trusted to continue those changes, should she not return to see them through herself.

She turned her attention to her belly, caressing it with her hands. With all she'd been through, the magic had nearly faded. For a time, she was afraid she'd lost them, but there was a hint of their essence still holding on, still fighting.

Though Liotha had never figured out how to transfer magic from Dro'Kal back into the world, she had studied enough transfer magic to figure out how to transfer magic between individuals. As such, she'd been slowly siphoning her own magic to fuel her children. The magic had limitations, so she couldn't be sure how well it would work, but she hoped it was enough for at least one to survive.

She was expecting to lay her eggs any day now. As soon as she did, she would leave. But before that happened, she needed to ensure her story would be passed on to her future heirs. And for that, she'd need Mother.

While she trusted Mother Ere'daina least of all her present advisors, Mother was the only one who knew Liotha's true story. If anyone was going to ensure Liotha's legacy continued, it had to be her. Mother owed her anyways. She just needed to convince the old dragoness it was the right thing to do.

Liotha lifted the letter off the table and folded it neatly, sliding it inside a nearby envelope. She grabbed the hot wax cup that had been warming over a candle and poured a dab onto the envelope's flap. Using the ring she'd been given on coronation day, she stamped and pressed the seal. The envelope was only to be opened by one of her own blood–or the future queen, should none of her offspring survive.

Leaving the letter sitting there, Liotha climbed into bed. She gazed at it one last time before blowing out the candle and drifting off to sleep. The days ahead would require much of her. She needed her rest now more than ever.

***

It was sometime midday when Liotha woke to a knocking sound. Wiping the sweat from her brow, she sat up in bed, instantly feeling the ache in her bones. She'd laid her eggs, six in count, just the day prior. She felt traces of magic in all of them, but feared it wasn't enough to see them break free from their shells. Her sleep had been filled with terrible visions borne of these fears.

She glanced over at the bed that had been prepared specially for her children as they awaited their hatching day. She smiled as she stared at them, basking in the hope of a world she tried to make better, for their sake.

The knocking came again. Someone was at her door.

"Come in," Liotha called out, sitting up and trying to fix her hair.

"Good morning, Queenmother," said the attendant whose face appeared in the cracked doorway. "Mother Ere'daina is here to see you, as requested."

"Very good. Send her in," Liotha replied. She would have preferred to meet Mother at a more proper time, and in a more proper place, but the doctors had told her she needed to rest for at least three days. As much as she didn't want to, with her task ahead, she agreed to give it two. She did need the rest, admittedly, so she conceded to have the Scion come visit her here.

Catching a glimpse of her guest through the cracked door, Liotha sat up even straighter and tried to make herself look as regal as possible. When dealing with Mother Ere'daina, she needed to be firm, now most especially.

"Thank you," Mother Ere'daina tipped her head to the attendant, who bowed in return and closed the door, leaving the two of them alone in the room. There was a short, awkward pause as the two stared at each other.

"How are you feeling?" Mother asked, averting her eyes to look about the room.

"I'm fine, but they told me I needed to rest."

"Yes, yes, standard protocol. Three days I've been told?"

"Yes, three."

"And the younglings, how are they?" Mother asked, her eyes spotting them resting off to the side.

"It remains to be seen. Their magic is weak. I did what I could, now the rest is up to them. Hopefully, at least one has the strength to emerge."

"Well, they are your children. I'm sure they'll do just fine." Mother smiled, but Liotha could tell it was merely a gesture.

"Yes. We'll see. Speaking of, that's why I called you here today. I have something important I need you to do."

"Me? Of course, my dear. Whatever the Queenmother commands of me." Mother bowed slightly, showing the proper respect. Liotha knew it was purely formality.

"You see that letter," Liotha said, nodding her head toward the desk.

"Yes."

"Take it. Keep it safe. It is for my children, should any of them survive. And if not, the future queen."

"Why are you giving it to me?" Mother asked, eyeing the letter curiously, then turning her attention back to Liotha.

"You are the only one who knows my true story. I do not trust you in many ways, but you are the only one I trust with this message. It does not reveal Dro'Kal's location, so don't even think about opening it yourself. That, I have hidden away, trusting that the right one will discover it and finish what I started. But this letter–it is the first step down the right path. It must *only* be opened by one of my blood, or the one to succeed me. You must swear, on your honor, that you will protect this message with your life."

"Yes, yes of course," Mother replied, her eyes staring intently at the letter for a few seconds. "So, you mean to go through with it then?"

"I told you I would set things right. It must be me."

"And there's nothing I can do to dissuade you?" Mother asked, sounding genuine for the first time in some time.

"No. I need to do this. It's not right, and it's eating me alive. I cannot sit on this throne a day longer without having at least tried to set things right. I've given my children their best chance to survive. Now, it's time I give the younglings who were sent to the humans theirs."

"Liotha, for what it's worth, I... am sorry. This is all my fault. At least take some of the Queensguard with you?"

"No. And you are right. It *is* your fault. That is why you will do this one last thing for me. I am serious about this, Mother. That letter is more important than we can both know. My story must be told. Our future queens need to know what almost happened here–what *did* happen, and what must happen still to set things right. If you want to atone for your sins, you will swear on the memory of Zareena–"

At the mention of the name, Mother's eyes shot up and her focus intensified.

"–swear that you will ensure my story is passed on. If ever you truly believed in Zareena, if ever you truly believed in me, you will see this one last task I am asking of you."

"Liotha, I– I have failed you in many ways. For that, I am so very sorry. But I will not fail you in this. You have my word."

Liotha stared into Mother's eyes for a long moment. She'd learned to read the deceitful dragoness quite well by now. And this time, it seemed, Mother was being genuinely sincere. As Liotha had hoped, the memory of Zareena was enough to ensure her cooperation. Because, at her core, Mother was still very much that young dragoness from all those cycles ago. She just hid behind her own masks so well it was so hard to see.

"Thank you, Mother," Liotha offered, truly relieved the matter was settled. It had been weighing on her more than anything else. "I think I'll rest some more now, if you don't mind."

"Of course, Queenmother. I'll leave you to it." Mother Ere'daina bowed graciously, a sincere, yet concerned smile directed at Liotha. "I'll see you after you're rested."

Liotha watched Mother leave, waiting for the door to close fully, leaving her alone in the room again. She sighed as she closed her eyes to rest again. *No, I don't think you will.*

Liotha's drifted toward sleep with her conscious more at ease. She'd come to terms with the last of what needed to be done. Now, she only needed to rest and prepare herself for the trials ahead. Whether she survived it or not was of little consequence. She only hoped her kind would remember her, not as their first queen, but as the queen who brought them out of darkness and into the light of a new dawn. And maybe, despite the monsters she'd created along the way, perhaps the rest of the world would come to know the steps she'd taken, and the sacrifices she'd made, to prevent all their annihilation. She couldn't know for sure, but she had to hope.

As the world faded to black, Liotha couldn't possibly have known just how pivotal her life would be. For, even as she was prepared to cast her own aside, it was the life within one of her eggs that would carry with it that seed of hope. This seed would pass from generation to generation, until the day Liotha's story would finally be fully revealed. And only then, amidst the world's darkest hour, would the true value of Liotha's life be wholly understood.

It was a new age, indeed. The dawn of the queen was merely just the beginning.

THANKS
...AND WHAT'S NEXT!

First, I'd like to take a quick second to offer one final "thank you" to any readers who've made it all the way through this book. You are amazing, and it means a lot to have you here with me. This is just the beginning, and we have an even wilder ride coming next. I hope you're ready!

Second, if you finished, I'll presume you enjoyed at least a good portion of it. If you have a few minutes, I'd really appreciate your honest review posted to your favorite platform of choice, though Amazon and Goodreads are the best places to start. The few minutes you spend writing that review will make a massive difference for this small-time indie author whose dream is the make this an eventual career. I plan to continue telling stories whether they sell or not, but at the end of the day, I'd prefer to focus on this gift and passion as a full-time job instead of a part-time hobby. Your reviews, in addition to sharing the book with others, can help me achieve that.

Lastly, I'd like to offer you an invitation. I've got a lot of books to write, and there are many opportunities for me to make them better as I go. If you're interested in being a part of that process as a beta reader, ARC reader, or just a general advocate for my world, I'd like to invite you to head on over to my website (https://join-the-awakening.com) and join the mailing list. Not only will it give you first access to news and writing updates, but you'll also get access to some freebies, the first of which was this prequel novella that you just read. If you missed out on that offer, I promise to try and provide more. If you've already read 'When Blood Burns', the debut novel, then hopefully this gave you greater insight into the world of Velasia, and possibly even answered some questions you were left with. If you haven't read the debut novel, then this should set you up nicely to better understand some of the events in that book and how it relates back to Velasia's clouded history.

Further books will continue to build upon these as we explore more and more of this fantasy world's rich history!

Until we continue the journey, I look forward to hearing from you and getting to know some of you as we explore this new, exciting world together!

The Awakening has finally begun...

COMMUNITY

If this book is your first venture into the Awakening, I'd like to extend you a quick invitation to join us online. Having a community can make a big difference, especially living in a world where loneliness and depression have become all too familiar. Besides just telling great stories, I want to build something that matters, and I can't do that without you. So, if you'd like to join us in this endeavor, the website should be your first stop. It will have all the information you need to become a true Seeker and member of our community.

Website: https://join-the-awakening.com

On the site, you'll not only find information about the world, along with news and updates about what's coming, but you'll also be presented with the choice of joining the newsletter. The newsletter will give you the deepest insight into what's happening and how the world of Velasia is coming to life. Being subscribed will also let you get the prequel novella 'Dawn of the Queen' for FREE, which is hopefully how you got this. There may be some other freebies in the future. I will strive to ensure giving me your email is well worth it on your part, as well as commit to not spamming you needlessly. You can expect one regular monthly update, and then occasional announcements like cover reveals and launch dates as necessary.

If you're familiar with Discord and want to join us there, we already have a small community started. Details are on the website, but if you want to dive right in now, here's the link to join. This will be where the majority of our community is built, but there may be other options in the future.

Discord: https://discord.gg/DRu2vZnBsz

I sincerely hope you'll join us in one form or another, and I look forward to meeting many of you in the near future!

AUTHOR
WHO I AM AND WHY I WROTE THIS BOOK

My name is Andrew Stevens, and I am many things. Husband, father, son, gamer, author, veteran. There is a lot more to me than just that, but those are the presiding words to describe what I am. But who I am, well, that's an entirely different question. I'm not sure I can answer it fully, but here's a brief attempt.

I am a creative, a dreamer. I am a wordsmith. I am a lover of stories, writing my own and even the occasional poetry. I am a searcher, always questioning the nature of my reality, always looking up to the stars, ever wondering what vast secrets lie beyond that which my eyes can see. I am a believer in a God who I will never claim to fully understand, yet trust to have my best interests in mind. I believe my gifts come from somewhere, and if not him, then where? I am an errant hopeful, always seeking the good in the world, though I still get discouraged when it seems hard to find.

I am all these and more. I am also a man who believes I can make the world a better place through my stories. And that brings us to why I wrote this book.

I wrote this book because it is something I must do. Writing and creating is a part of me that I didn't realize to its fullest for many years. Once I found the means and the will to see it through, the result is the blood, sweat, and tears you have just read. It's not perfect, but like my soul, it is deeply intertwined with who I am. It is a mirror—a brief glimpse into the reflection of my deepest self.

Whether the words resonate with you or not, I appreciate you taking a chance. I appreciate your willingness to invest some of life's most precious resource into me and the past few years of my life. At the end of the day, no matter how you feel about it, know I am eternally grateful.

However, if you do find the words, characters, and events provide some level of meaning into your own life, I'd ask only one favor of you. Would you kindly leave an honest review on your favorite platform? As an author, especially an indie author, reviews are the lifeblood of my work. It may seem a simple thing to you, but it means the world to me.

Again, thank you for your time, and if you've made it this far, you given me much more than I deserve. Hopefully, the pages have at least reinvested some of that gift back to you. From the bottom of my heart, I sincerely hope so.

Cheers,
Andrew Stevens

Shadows stir, the world trembles.

Steel yourselves, Seekers.

The Awakening has begun...

https://join-the-awakening.com